1本就通！日常英文表達大小事

姜鎮豪、卞惠允 ── 著
Emma Feng ── 譯

全書MP3一次下載

http://booknews.com.tw/mp3/9786269793938.htm

全 MP3 一次下載為 zip 壓縮檔
部分智慧型手機須安裝解壓縮程式方可開啟。iOS 系統請升級至 iOS 13 以上。
此為大型檔案，建議使用 WIFI 連線下載，以免占用流量，並確認連線狀況，以利下載順暢。

請簡單回答一下這個問題：
「我是不是能夠用英文表達日常生活中的大小事？」

一般人早上起床後，要做好外出的準備，然後往學校或工作地點去。晚上回到家後休息，然後準備迎接明天的生活，最後就寢入睡，結束這一天。在週末假日或休假時，有人會去旅行、外出約會等，有人則會參加自己宗教相關或其他類型的活動。

我們在這一連串的過程中展現出來的生活模式，可能成為聊天、對話或寫作的題材。如果您仔細回想與朋友之間的對話，也許你會更清楚這一點。你是否經常與母語人士對話呢？在週末假日時，若有機會和外國人聊天時，你們的話題會圍繞著做過的事情或發生過的事情吧！因此，學習用英文來聊聊自己的日常生活大小事吧！透過這樣的互動與交流的同時，我們也會從對方說的話語當中增加自己的語言能力與知識，且人際關係也逐漸建立起來。因此，學習日常生活用語的表達能力，絕對是彼此更深層交流的寶貴開端，我們絕不能忽視它的重要性。

正因為我們明白這是很重要的一點，所以我們在這本「1本就通！日常英文表達大小事》」中，藉由一般人日常生活的樣態，以及在週末假日、假期的各種情境，教您如何用簡短的英語來表達生活中的大小事。

　　學習這樣的日常生活表達用語，比其他任何表達用語更重要的原因是，我們在學習過程中會感受到一種「用熟悉事物來學習一種語言」的樂趣。因為，要任何的學習要能夠持之以恆的話，就必須在過程中帶有一點樂趣和愉快。當你開始試著用英語來表達自己熟悉的事物時，原本看似困難且神秘的英文，就變得與你更親近些了。而這正是讓學習英語持續下去的關鍵點。

　　早上醒來時不經意地關掉鬧鐘，用英語該怎麼說？將麥片倒進碗裡，再倒入牛奶，英文怎麼說？從捷運站出口刷卡出來，用英文如何表達？如果這些以前沒學過、沒想過要怎麼表達的用語湧入你的腦海，且讓你渴望試著表達和分享，那麼這本書就是讓你精進的好教材了。相信接下來你會不知不覺地掌握許多表達用語，在口語的表達上也會越來越流利。

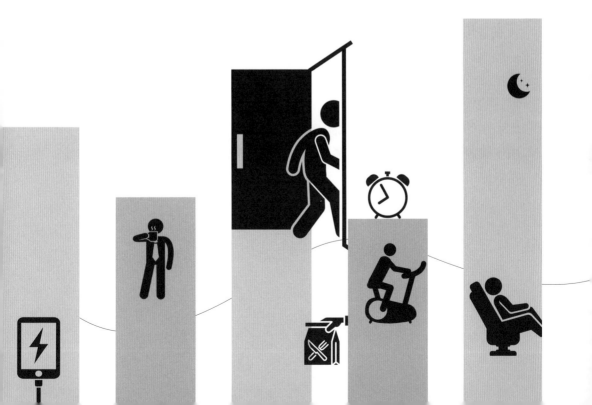

本書的架構及使用方式

　　本書整理了一般人日常生活中，從早上起床一直到晚間就寢一整天中，最常表現出的行為、最常見的狀態，並教你如何用最到的說法來表達。當然，或許有些人過著比較不一樣的生活，但仍可利用本書彙整的日常用語，好好理解來增進本身的英文實力。

　　你不需要從第一頁開始閱讀、學習，可以從任何一個章節或一個小單元開始，或者你可以透過本書的目錄，從自己感興趣，或即將遇到的情境開始。重要的是不放棄與堅持。「我要一週內讀完這本書」或「我要在一個月內讀三遍」，與其有這樣的期許，不如每天至少讀一頁，維持每日學習的熱度，千萬別錯過任何一天。持之以恆地學習，就像滴水穿石一樣，你會發現之前不容易記住的東西也會漸漸刻劃在腦海裡，而當你看到其他情境的英文句子或類似的內容時，你會更明確地掌握一些用語。

　　在每個單元的學習中，建議你先閱讀中文表達用語，然後試著想想如何用英語來說，然後再查看書中的英語表達。一開始可以只用眼睛看，第二次可以大聲讀出來，第三次可以掃描 QR 碼，跟著模仿發音及語調。這樣的學習方法會有很好的效果。當你覺得學習有一定程度的進展時，試著看著索引中的中文詞彙並用英文說出來，再看著英文表達用語，用中文說出它們的意思，這樣的訓練會讓你完全掌握這些日常表達用語。

《1本就通！日常英文表達大小事》旨在幫助學習者提升口語會話及文字書寫的表達能力，其內容架構如下：

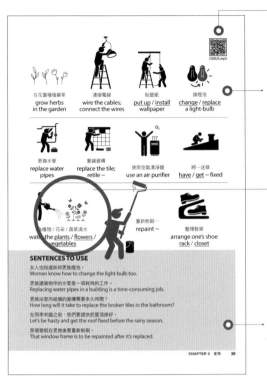

附QR碼線上音檔，全書日常生活英文短語的表達，以及 SENTENCES TO USE中的例句，皆由道地口音的母語人士錄製，讓您學習最精確的發音。

change / replace a light-bulb是指 change a light-bulb 以及 replace a light-bulb 是一樣的意思，所以只有一個中文解釋「換燈泡」。而不同字彙的替換表達也都有錄音。

而 water the plants / flowers / vegetables 這類用語是指在 water the 後面，可以用不同的單字來套用替換，所以從「為植物／花朵／蔬菜澆水」的解釋也可一覽無遺。同樣，water the plants、water the flowers、water the vegetables也都有錄音。

頁面下方 SENTENCES TO USE 示範幾句該頁學過的用語如何用於實際生活會話或書面表達中。

提供會話範例，進一步引導讀者如何將之前學過的表達用語，運用於實際生活中。同時，這些 120% 逼真、生動的情境會話也將為您的學習增添樂趣。

當你認為自己已經學習到一個程度，或者有臨時的需要時，可以利用後面以英文字母順序編排、中英對照的索引，迅速找到臨時需要的一句話，這會讓實際運用更有效率，並讓你的口語表達更為流利。

目錄

CHAPTER 1 起床後 AFTER GETTING UP

CHAPTER 2 家務 HOUSEWORK

CHAPTER 3 交通 TRANSPORTATION

CHAPTER 4 地方 PLACES

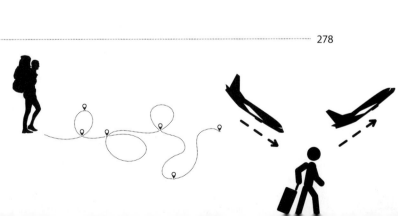

CHAPTER

1

起床後

AFTER GETTING UP

1 起床

鬧鐘響起
the alarm clock <u>goes off</u> / <u>rings</u>

在床上翻來覆去
<u>turn</u> / <u>roll</u> over in bed

按下「貪睡」按鈕
（幾分鐘後鬧鐘會再次響起的計時器按鈕）
hit the snooze button

關掉鬧鐘
turn off the alarm clock

打開收音機
turn on the radio

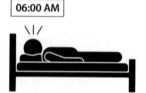

早上6點起床
wake up at 6 a.m.

SENTENCES TO USE

一大早聽到鬧鐘響起時，他就在床上翻來覆去。
He turned over in bed as the alarm went off in the early morning.

我通常早上7點起床準備上班，但我週末會睡晚一點。
I usually wake up at 7 a.m. for work, but I sleep in on the weekends.

C01U1_1.mp3

睡意未醒，半夢半醒
be half asleep

一大早就起床
get up in the early morning

SAT 11:00 AM

週末晚起床
get up late on (the) weekends

from 9 PM to 6 AM

熬夜
stay up all night; pull an all-nighter

（無意間）睡過頭
oversleep

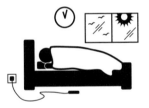

（不尋常地／刻意）睡過頭
sleep in

她整堂課都在半夢半醒中度過。
She was half asleep throughout the whole class.

我熬夜準備今天的小測驗。
I pulled an all-nighter preparing for the quiz today.

我今天睡過頭，而且上學遲到了。
I overslept today and I am late for school.

（從床上起身後）坐在床上伸懶腰
sit up in bed and stretch

戴上眼鏡
put one's glasses on

下床
get out of bed

整理床鋪
make one's bed

整理被褥；摺棉被
fold up the bedding

開燈
turn on the light

開窗戶
open the window

望向外面
look outside

SENTENCES TO USE

起床後坐在床上伸個懶腰，這是開始一天的美好方式。
Sitting up in bed and stretching is a good way to start the day.

我在離開房間前都會整理床鋪。
I always make my bed before I leave my room.

在冬天早上我不會把窗戶打開。
We don't open the windows in mornings during the winter.

C01U1_2.mp3

查看電子郵件
check one's email

查看手機訊息
check text messages on one's mobile phone

穿上浴袍
put on a shower robe

穿上運動服／慢跑服裝
put on one's <u>sportswear</u> / <u>jogging suit</u>

離開房間
<u>get out of</u> / <u>leave</u>
one's room

打開／看新聞報導
<u>turn on</u> / <u>check</u> the news

我習慣在早上查看公司的電子郵件。
I have a habit of checking my business emails in the morning.

請穿上浴袍吧。你把地板都淋濕了。
Please put on a shower robe. You are dripping all over the floor.

C01U1_PU.mp3

A　親愛的，起床囉！已經早上7點30分了。
▶ Honey, wake up! It's already 7:30 a.m.

B　喔…我想再多睡一會兒。
● Argh… I wish I could sleep in a little.

A　你會遲到的。你睡得好嗎？
▶ You are going to be late. Did you sleep well?

B　沒有，我一整晚都沒睡好。現在全身僵硬。而且我昨晚做了個不安寧的夢。那你呢？
● No, I had a bad night. My whole body feels stiff. And I had a disturbing dream last night. How about you?

A　我睡得非常好。你要遲到了，先去梳洗一下吧。
▶ I slept very well. You are late, so go freshen up first.

我得馬上去準備早餐了。
▶ I am going to make breakfast right away.

B　好的。我快一點就不會遲到了。
● Alright, I won't be late if I hurry.

早上問候
早安（您好）！
Morning!
Good morning!

今天早上還好嗎？
How are you this morning?
How is your morning so far?

祝你有美好的一天。
Good day to you.

各種「睡得好」的表達用語。
I slept well / soundly.
I had a good night (sleep).
I had a good night's sleep.
I had a fine night.
I got enough sleep.

2 晨間運動

C01U2.mp3

去慢跑
go jogging

做運動
do a workout;
work out

帶寵物去散步
take one's pet for
a walk

走在步道上
walk the trails

在公園散步
take a walk
in the park

去健身房
go to the <u>gym</u> / <u>fitness</u>
<u>center</u>; hit the gym
（gym:健身房）

去游泳
go
swimming

去登山
go
(mountain) hiking

* stretch 可以當名詞
也可以當動詞。

進行伸展（運動）
stretch

做瑜伽
do yoga

跳繩
<u>skip</u> / <u>jump</u> rope

騎單車
ride a bicycle

SENTENCES TO USE

傑克每天早上都去遛狗。
Jake takes his dog for a walk every morning.

下班後你想去健身房運動嗎？
Do you want to go to the gym and work out after work?

我週末時都會去登山。
I go hiking on the weekends.

我以伸展運動和瑜伽展開我的一天。
I start the day with a stretch and yoga.

我弟弟曾經每天晚上做跳繩運動。
My brother used to jump rope every evening to exercise.

A　啊嗚… 我感覺我還在半夢半醒之中。我得做點拉伸的運動。
▶ Argh… It feels like I am still half asleep. I need to stretch a little.

B　米婭小姐，妳今早好嗎？
你又一早就出來運動了呢。
● How are you this morning, Mia? You are out early to exercise again.

A　早啊，史密斯先生。你每天早上都帶著你的狗去慢跑，真了不起。
▶ Good morning, Mr. Smith. It's amazing that you jog with your dog every morning.

B　別說了！我們家這隻狗，每天一大早五點半就把我叫起來出去散步，我是沒辦法只好出來了。
● Tell me about it! I can't help but come out when my dog wakes me up every 5:30 a.m. to go out for a walk.

A　這小傢伙真是勤奮呢！也許這就是牠看起來像你一樣健康的原因吧，史密斯先生。
▶ This guy is very diligent! Maybe that's why your dog looks as healthy as you, Mr. Smith.

B　的確。我在周圍看到很多狗狗因為生病必須經常去醫院，但我很開心我這隻狗是健康的。
● True. I see a lot of dogs around me that visit the vet often due to illness, but I'm glad my dog is healthy.

A　你的狗幾歲了？
▶ How old is your dog?

B　牠8歲了。以人的年齡算的話，相當於60歲左右吧。跟我的年紀差不多。
● He is 8 years old. About 60 in human age. Similar to my age.

A 我以為他大概是約2到3歲,因為他看起來很結實,但他比我所想的年紀要大。
▶ I thought he would be around 2~3 because he looks strong, but he is older than I thought.

他看起來和史密斯先生一樣年輕。哈哈。
▶ He looks as youthful as Mr. Smith. Haha.

B 哦,我的天,這真是太誇獎了!祝你有個愉快的一天,下次見。
● Oh my, what a compliment! Have a good day and see you next time.

A 也祝你有愉快的一天。
▶ Have a nice day, too.

去上廁所
go to the bathroom

使用免治馬桶
use a bidet

沖馬桶
flush the toilet

脫下睡衣
take off one's sleepwear

穿上拖鞋
put on slippers

洗洗手
wash one's hands

洗洗臉
wash one's face

SENTENCES TO USE

使用免治馬桶是我每天早上例行事務的重要部分之一。
Using a bidet is a vital part of my morning routine.

早餐前請別忘了洗手。
Don't forget to wash your hands before breakfast.

C01U3_1.mp3

沖澡；淋浴
<u>take</u> / <u>have</u> a shower

洗澡
<u>take</u> / <u>have</u> a bath

用洗髮精洗頭髮
wash one's hair
with shampoo

用護髮素保養頭髮
condition one's hair;
use a conditioner

刮鬍子
shave

刷牙
brush one's teeth

莎拉用洗髮精洗頭後並沒有用護髮素。
Sarah does not use a conditioner after she washes her hair with shampoo.

他出門上班前忘記刮鬍子了。
He forgot to shave before he left for work.

我通常在淋浴時刷牙。
I usually brush my teeth while I take a shower.

（用杯水）漱口
rinse out one's mouth

漱口
gargle

擤鼻涕
blow one's nose

挖鼻孔
pick one's nose

用棉花棒挖耳朵
pick one's ears
with a cotton swab

在臉上擦拭一些爽膚水 / 乳液 / 乳霜
apply / put on some toner /
lotion / cream on one's face

SENTENCES TO USE

我在沖完澡後用棉花棒挖耳朵。
I pick my ears with a cotton swab after taking a shower.

我總是用棉花棒塗抹眼霜。
I always apply eye cream with a cotton swab.

吹乾頭髮
dry one's hair

梳頭髮
comb one's hair

整理頭髮
do one's hair

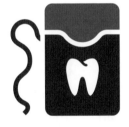

化妝
put on one's makeup;
put one's makeup on

使用牙線
floss; use a floss

我姪女每天早上都很討厭梳理她的頭髮。
My niece hates combing her hair every morning.

漢娜在去重要約會之前整理了她的頭髮。
Hannah did her hair before she went off to an important appointment.

在吹乾頭髮後我還得化妝。
I need to put my makeup on after drying my hair.

牙醫建議刷牙後使用牙線。
Dentists recommend using a floss after brushing teeth.

4 早餐

準備早餐
prepare breakfast

不吃早餐
skip breakfast

吃早餐
eat / have breakfast

經由濾水器倒出水
pour water from
the water purifier

削水果皮
peel / skin the fruit

* oil 當動詞，表示
「澆上油」

在煎鍋上抹油
oil the frying pan

將蛋打入鍋中
crack an egg into the pan

烤土司
make toast

在麵包上抹些果醬
spread some jam on bread

SENTENCES TO USE

媽媽在準備早餐的同時，爸爸在泡咖啡。
My father makes coffee while my mother prepares breakfast.

媽媽從不讓我不吃早餐。
My mother never lets me skip breakfast.

務必記得蛋打進去之前鍋底要抹油。
Always remember to oil the pan before cracking an egg into it.

對我來說，做吐司是最簡單的餐點。
Making toast is the simplest meal for me.

我喜歡在麵包上抹草莓果醬，而不是藍莓果醬。
I like to spread strawberry jam instead of blueberry jam on my bread.

從冰箱拿一些配菜出來
get some side dishes out of the refrigerator

煮飯和煮湯
cook rice and soup

沖泡咖啡
brew / make coffee

將穀片倒進碗裡
pour cereal into the bowl

將牛奶倒進穀片碗裡
pour milk into the cereal bowl

將飯菜放在微波爐中加熱
heat up the rice in the microwave

擺餐桌
set the table

與⋯分享食物
share food with ~

準備某人的午餐便當
pack one's lunch / brown bag; prepare one's lunch box

SENTENCES TO USE

請把一些配菜拿出來放在餐桌上。
Please get some side dishes out on the table.

我先把穀片倒進碗裡，再把牛奶倒下去。
I pour cereal into the bowl before pouring milk.

我對於早上用微波爐加熱飯菜感到厭倦了。
I am sick of heating up rice in the microwave in the morning.

你能把早餐的餐桌擺置好嗎？
Could you set the table for breakfast?

今天你不必準備自己的便當。
You don't have to pack your lunch today.

A 兒子，我稍後會清理，把你的碗放在水槽裡就行了。
▶ Son, I will clean up later, so put your bowl in the sink.

B 好的，媽媽。我現在要去洗臉洗手一下。
● Okay, mom. I am going to wash up now.

A 你要遲到了。趕快去換衣服、穿上襪子，還有刷牙。
▶ You're late. Hurry up and change, put on your socks and brush your teeth.

B 哎呀，我忘記整理我的書包了。
● Oh, I forgot to pack my backpack.

A 你睡覺前就該整理好了。
▶ You should have packed it before you went to bed.

那你的作業呢？
▶ How about your homework?

B 是的，媽媽。作業我昨天就做完了。
● Yeah, mom. I finished it yesterday.

A 好。別忘了帶便當。
▶ Good. Don't forget your lunch box.

B 好的，媽媽，我走了。
● Okay. See you later, mom.

A 嗯，好好聽老師的話，不要和朋友吵架，在學校玩得開心點喔。
▶ Yes, listen to your teachers, don't get into trouble with your friends, and have fun at school.

英文裡與「蛋」有關的餐點

Hotel chef **How would you like your eggs?**
您的蛋要怎麼煮呢？

Me 「我該怎麼說好呢？我只知道煎蛋耶。」

在國外的飯店或餐廳聽到這句話的時候，我們是否曾經感到徬徨？蛋類根據不同的烹飪方法，有多種表達方式。現在讓我們一一學習。

raw egg: 生蛋

egg white(s): 蛋白

egg yolk: 蛋黃

soft boiled: （半熟的）蒸煮蛋

hard boiled: （全熟的）蒸煮蛋

poached:
（用滾燙熱水烹煮的）水煮蛋

omelet:
煎蛋卷（打散的蛋液，夾帶著起司、肉類、蔬菜等內餡）

scrambled:
（將蛋打開混攪成蛋液後做成的）炒蛋

fried eggs: 煎蛋

> 注意　「日式蛋包飯」（omurice）是源自於日本語的食物，正確的英文寫法是 "omelet"。

各種煎蛋類型（由上到下熟度增加）

sunny-side-up:
單面熟，蛋黃微微鼓起的煎蛋

over easy:
雙面熟，只略煮蛋白的煎蛋

over hard:
雙面全熟，包括蛋黃都炒熟的煎蛋

Example

Q: How would you like your eggs?
您的蛋想怎麼煮呢？

A: I would like my eggs **over easy**, please.
我想要半熟的煎蛋，謝謝。

Can I get a ham and cheese **omelet**?
我可以要一份火腿起司芝士煎蛋嗎？

I'll get two **hard boiled eggs** with the bacon.
我要兩顆全熟的蒸煮蛋，再加培根。

I'd like mine **scrambled**, please.
我要炒蛋，謝謝。

Poached egg on the side would be great!
可以另外加個水煮蛋就太好了。

* put on 強調的是「穿衣」這個動作，而 wear 是指「穿著衣服」的狀態。

穿上／穿著…；穿上衣服
<u>put on</u> / <u>wear</u> ~;
get dressed

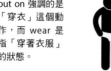

穿上／著內衣
<u>put on</u> / <u>wear</u>
underwear

穿上／著襯衫
<u>put on</u> / <u>wear</u>
a shirt

穿上／著絲襪
<u>put on</u> / <u>wear</u>
one's stockings

穿褲子
<u>put on</u> / <u>wear</u>
a pair of pants

穿裙子
<u>put on</u> / <u>wear</u> a
skirt

拉上…的拉鍊
zip up ~

繫上腰帶
wear a belt

穿襪子
<u>put on</u> / <u>wear</u> some socks

打領帶
<u>put on</u> / <u>wear</u> a tie

調整領帶
<u>fix</u> / <u>straighten</u> one's tie

SENTENCES TO USE

我應該先穿上裙子嗎？還是要先穿絲襪呢？
Do I have to put on a skirt first? or stockings first?

別忘了把褲子拉鍊拉上來。 Don't forget to zip up your pants.

請繫上腰帶，不然褲子會滑落。 Please wear a belt before your pants roll down.

我每次打領帶都會覺得不舒服。 I feel uncomfortable whenever I wear a tie.

照鏡子調整好你的領帶。 Look into the mirror and fix your tie.

C01U5.mp3

翻找櫥櫃／抽屜
rummage through one's
<u>wardrobe</u> / <u>drawer</u>

扣上…的鈕扣
button (up) ~

解開…的鈕扣
unbutton ~

戴上手套
<u>put on</u> / <u>wear</u>
one's gloves

整理好背包
pack one's backpack

穿上鞋子
<u>put on</u> / <u>wear</u> one's shoes

把所有燈都關掉
turn off all the lights

關上門並鎖好
close the door and lock it

走出家門；離開家
<u>leave</u> / <u>get out of</u>
the house

SENTENCES TO USE

別翻找抽屜了！你的襪子就在這裡。
Stop rummaging through your drawer! Your socks are right here.

孩子們常沒辦法把襯衫的鈕扣扣上。
Children frequently have trouble buttoning up their shirts.

我們在沙灘上不必穿鞋。
We don't have to wear shoes on the beach.

務必關掉所有電燈，然後把門關上並鎖好。
Make sure to turn off all the lights before closing and locking the door.

可以麻煩你早上離開這房子，好讓我清理一下嗎？
Do you mind leaving the house in the morning, so I can clean up?

CHAPTER

2

家務

HOUSEWORK

清潔

洗碗盤
do the dishes

收拾桌子
clear the table

清理廚房
clean up the kitchen

整理房間
tidy up the room

讓房間通風
air out / ventilate
the room

將東西歸位
put one's things
away

清除家具上的灰塵
dust
the furniture

用吸塵器清理地板
vacuum
the floor

擦窗戶
wipe the window

拖地
mop the floor

刷馬桶 / 洗手臺 / 浴缸
scrub the toilet / sink / bathtub

SENTENCES TO USE

收拾桌子後洗碗盤。
Do the dishes after clearing the table.

如果你不打算幫忙做家務，至少你可以整理一下你的房間！
If you are not going to help around the house, you can at least tidy up your room!

把你的玩具收起來，不然我直接扔掉。
Put your toys away, or I will just throw them away.

在用吸塵器吸地板之前，我們應該先為家具除塵。
Let's dust the furniture before we vacuum the floor.

這間浴室真髒！你多久沒有刷洗了？
This bathroom is so dirty! How long has it been since you scrubbed it?

清除霉菌
clean off / remove
the mold

倒垃圾
take out the trash /
garbage

將可回收垃圾做分類
separate / sort the recyclable
waste / recyclables

在庭院掃地
sweep the yard

在花園除草
weed the garden

預約 / 聯絡清潔服務
book / call a
cleaning service

整理某人的物品
organize one's things

清理冰箱
clean out the fridge;
clean the refrigerator

用機器人吸塵器清掃地板
a robot vacuum cleans
the floor

SENTENCES TO USE

你唯一的家務就是倒垃圾，而你都沒做。
Your only chore was to take out the trash and you didn't do it.

將可回收垃圾分類有助於環境保護，這是必要的事。
It is imperative to separate the recyclables to help the environment.

我會固定預約清潔服務，因為我外出工作的時間很長。
I regularly book a cleaning service, since I work outside the house a lot.

哎呀！你去度假前都沒有清理冰箱嗎？
Oh no! You didn't clean out the fridge before you left for your vacation?

我朋友帶了一部用來清掃地板的機器人吸塵器，作為入厝的送禮。
My friend brought a robot vacuum as a housewarming gift to clean the floor.

將衣物分類（依顏色 / 材質）
sort out the laundry
(by <u>color</u> / <u>fabric</u>)

在洗衣前先將襯衫浸泡在水中
soak the shirt in water before washing;
pre-soak the shirt before washing

將衣物放入洗衣機中
put the laundry
in the washing machine

將衣物柔軟劑加入洗衣機中
add the fabric softener
into the washing machine

將衣物掛起晾乾
hang the laundry
up to dry

將衣物放入烘乾機 / 以烘乾模式讓衣物乾燥
<u>put the laundry in the dryer</u> / <u>tumble dry
the laundry</u>

SENTENCES TO USE

每個人在洗衣服之前都得依顏色將待洗衣物做分類。
Everyone needs to sort out their laundry by color before washing them.

毛衣不應放入烘衣機中，因為這樣會縮水。
Sweaters should not be put in the dryer because it will shrink.

摺衣服
fold the clothes

燙衣服
iron the clothes

整理衣物
organize clothes

重新整理衣櫥
rearrange one's wardrobe

將衣物送到洗衣店／乾洗店
take one's clothes to the
cleaner's / dry cleaner's

從洗衣店／乾洗店取回衣物
pick up one's clothes from
the cleaner's / dry cleaner's

使用立式蒸氣熨斗／蒸氣衣櫥來照料衣物
take care of one's clothes with
a standing steam iron / a steam closet

彼得在週末時會自己熨燙他所有的襯衫。
Peter irons all of his shirts himself on the weekend.

我習慣每年春天會重整我的衣櫥。
I have a habit of rearranging my wardrobe every spring.

我用蒸氣衣櫥來照料我所有的針織衣物。
I take care of all my knit wears with my steam closet.

A 親愛的，今天是春季大掃除的好日子啊。
▶ Honey, it's a perfect day for spring cleaning today.

B 當然，讓我們一起將這骯髒的房子打掃得乾乾淨淨吧。
● Sure, let's make this dirty house look spick and span.

A 我用吸塵器把地板吸乾淨後，你就可以把地板拖乾淨了。
▶ You can mop the floor clean once I vacuum the floor.

B 好的。在此之前，我想我們應該先處理床上和衣櫃裡的一堆舊衣服。
● Okay. Before that, I think we should take care of the worn clothes all over the bed and the closet.

A 我們把所有衣物集中起來，放進洗衣機中，然後加些洗滌劑和織物柔軟劑。
▶ Let's collect all the laundry, put it in the washing machine with some detergent and fabric softener.

B 我們要把被子拿到投幣式洗衣店洗嗎？
● Are we going to wash our comforters at the coin laundry?

A 是的，這些被子很大。所以，我打算在那裡清洗並用烘衣機烘乾。
▶ Yes, the comforters are big. So, I am going to wash it there and use the dryer as well.

B 哇，好多灰塵啊！我去把窗戶打開，撣去灰塵。
● Wow, there is a lot of dust! I'm going to open the window and dust it off.

A 是的，然後我最好還是得用吸塵器清一下。
▶ Yeah, I'd better vacuum after that.

B 我應該把所有乾的衣物摺好放進衣櫃嗎？
● Should I fold all the dry laundry and put it in the closet?

A 是的，但是乾毛巾應該放在浴室裡。
  ▶ Yes, but the dried towels should be put in the bathroom.

B 我們來把所有垃圾做分類，然後放到外面。
  ● Let's separate all the trash and put it outside.

（一個小時後 In an hour）

A 哇！我們的房子真是乾淨。你做得很棒！
  ▶ Wow! Our house is so clean. Well done.

B 你也是，親愛的！
  ● You too, Honey!

支付（水電費）帳單
pay one's (utility) bills

記錄家庭開銷
keep records of household
expenses; use an account book

開啟 / 關閉暖爐
turn <u>on</u> / <u>off</u> the heater

開啟 / 關閉加濕器
turn <u>on</u> / <u>off</u> the
humidifier

開啟 / 關閉除濕機
turn <u>on</u> / <u>off</u> the
dehumidifier

租借家用電器
rent a home
appliance

修理屋子
repair one's house

重新裝修屋子
<u>renovate</u> / <u>redecorate</u>
one's house

安裝壁爐 / 淋浴間
install <u>a fireplace</u> /
<u>a shower stall</u> (or booth)

打電話給建商
call a constructor

打電話給維修工
call a repairman

SENTENCES TO USE

你得繳瓦斯費，不然你就沒辦法煮飯了。
You need to pay your gas bills or you won't be able to cook.

潘姆非常仔細地記錄家庭開銷方面。
Pam is meticulous in keeping records of household expenses.

這裡很潮濕！我們關掉加濕器，打開除濕機吧。
It's humid in here! Let's turn off the humidifier and turn on the dehumidifier.

為了讓浴室寬敞些，莉莉計畫拆掉浴缸，然後打造一個淋浴間。
Lily plans to remove the tub and install a shower stall for a spacious bathroom.

我打算打電話一家建商，要重新裝修我的房屋並安裝一個壁爐。
I am going to call a constructor to renovate my house and install a fireplace.

C02U3.mp3

在花園種植藥草
grow herbs
in the garden

連接電線
wire the cables;
connect the wires

貼壁紙
put up / install
wallpaper

換燈泡
change / replace
a light-bulb

更換水管
replace water
pipes

重鋪瓷磚
replace the tile;
retile ~

使用空氣清淨器
use an air purifier

將…送修
have / get ~ fixed

為植物 / 花朵 / 蔬菜澆水
water the plants / flowers /
vegetables

重新粉刷…
repaint ~

整理鞋架
arrange one's shoe
rack / closet

SENTENCES TO USE

女人也知道如何更換燈泡。
Women know how to change the light-bulb too.

更換建築物中的水管是一項耗時的工作。
Replacing water pipes in a building is a time-consuming job.

更換浴室內破損的瓷磚需要多久時間？
How long will it take to replace the broken tiles in the bathroom?

在雨季來臨之前，我們要趕快把屋頂修好。
Let's be hasty and get the roof fixed before the rainy season.

那個窗框在更換後要重新粉刷。
That window frame is to be repainted after it's replaced.

A 你想怎麼裝修你的室內空間呢？
▶ How would you like your interior done?

B 首先，我想把這面牆拆掉，讓客廳可以更大些。
● First, I want this wall torn for a bigger living room.

然後我想在露台和客廳之間安裝一扇滑動式玻璃門。
● And I also want a glass sliding door installed between the terrace and the living room.

A 好的。然後你想將這櫃子擺在右邊角落處是嗎？
▶ Okay. And you want the cabinet on the right corner, right?

B 沒錯。但請不要將櫃子安置的位置太靠近冷氣機。
● That's right. But please install the cabinet not too close to the air conditioner.

A 那廚房呢？
▶ How about the kitchen?

B 請用白色系的環保材料替換水槽。
● Please replace the sink with a white-toned eco-friendly material.

A 我該把這咖啡桌組附著在牆邊嗎？
▶ Should I build the island table attached to the wall?

B 是的，麻煩了。且要用大理石來做料理枱。
● Yes, please. And make the countertop out of marble.

A 浴室裡面要做個淋浴間並更換馬桶嗎？
▶ Should I install a shower stall and replace the toilet in the bathroom?

B 是的，另外，別忘了依照我說過形狀來鋪磁磚。
● Yes, and additionally, don't forget to construct the tiles in the shape I mentioned.

C02U3_PU.mp3

A　沒問題。那麼壁紙和燈飾呢？
▶ No problem. What about the wallpaper and the lighting?

B　壁紙請使用 W2103 型號的，且客廳要掛一個吊燈。
● Use the W2103 model for the wallpaper and a chandelier will be hung in the living room.

其餘的部分請使用普通的 30W LED 燈泡。
● Please use regular 30W LED lamps for the rest.

A　好的。還需要其他吩咐嗎？
▶ Okay. Do you need anything else?

B　是的。需要多久時間，以及費用是多少？
● Yup. How long will it take and how much will it cost?

A　等我將工期和費用估算整理好後，會發一封電子郵件給您。
▶ I will send you an email after organizing the estimate of the construction period and the cost.

哺乳／用奶瓶餵養
（某人的嬰兒）
breastfeed /
bottle-feed (one's baby)

餵嬰兒吃東西
feed baby food

換尿布
change one's diaper

消毒嬰兒用品
disinfect baby
supplies

訓練走路；教導嬰兒行走
train one's steps;
teach a baby to walk

訓練孩子坐馬桶
potty-train / toilet
train one's child

與孩子互動
interact with
one's child

將孩子放進嬰兒推車
put a child in a
stroller

帶著孩子去散步
take a walk with
one's child

唱催眠曲
sing a lullaby

安撫焦躁不安的孩子
soothe a fussy /
an upset child

哄孩子入睡；讓孩子小睡一下
put ~ to sleep;
put ~ down for a nap

SENTENCES TO USE

嬰兒通常會先餵母奶或以奶瓶餵奶，之後會吃副食品。
Babies are usually breastfed or bottlefed before eating solid foods.

有些媽媽對於嬰兒要觸碰的每樣東西會特別做消毒。
Some mothers are very particular about disinfecting everything her baby touches.

在孩子上幼稚園之前，訓練孩子坐馬桶非常重要。
It is important to potty-train your child before they go to kindergarten.

我喜歡把我的寶寶放在嬰兒推車裡，然後帶他出去散步。
I like to put my baby in a stroller and take a walk with him.

他今天似乎很煩躁。為什麼不讓他小睡一下呢？
He seems very fussy today. Why don't you put him down for a nap?

送孩子去托育中心
take ~ to a
daycare center

送孩子去幼兒園
send ~ to
kindergarten

去親子咖啡廳
go to a kids cafe

在親子咖啡廳和孩子一起玩
play with a child
at a kids cafe

分享育兒資訊
share parenting
information

接受育兒諮詢
receive childcare
counseling

讓孩子接種疫苗
get one's child
vaccinated

（為孩子）做定期健康檢查
have / get a regular
checkup (for one's child)

為孩子準備餐點／點心
prepare a child's meal /
snack

讚揚孩子的好行為
praise one's
good behavior

管教孩子
discipline ~

SENTENCES TO USE

我以前帶女兒去托育中心時她經常會嚎啕大哭。
My daughter used to wail when I took her to the daycare center.

每次在親子咖啡廳和孩子玩耍時，會累的往往是我自己。
Whenever I play with a child at a kids cafe, I am the one who gets exhausted.

媽媽可以帶著孩子去親子咖啡廳，且在孩子玩耍時彼此交流育兒資訊。
A mother can go to a kids cafe with her child and share parenting information while the kids play.

如果你覺得兒子似乎發育落後，你應該接受育兒諮詢。
You should receive childcare counseling if you feel like your son seems underdeveloped.

定期為孩子做健康檢查及接種疫苗是相當重要的。
It is vital to get a regular checkup and get one's child vaccinated.

寵物做伴

給寵物餵食
feed one's pet; <u>feed</u>
/ <u>give</u> food to one's pet

擺置尿墊
lay out <u>pads</u>
/ <u>potty-pads</u>

將髒了的尿墊換掉
change dirty <u>pads</u>
/ <u>potty-pads</u>

套上牽繩
put on a leash

給⋯（寵物）戴上口絡
put a muzzle on

將寵物排泄物裝入塑膠袋中
pack the pet poop in a plastic bag

SENTENCES TO USE

吉米總是給他年老的貓餵食高檔的有機寵物食品。
Jim always feeds high-grade organic pet food to his elderly cat.

帶寵物出去散步前，別忘了套上牽繩。
Don't forget to put on a leash before taking your pet out for a walk.

要是一隻狗在街上試圖吃任何東西，主人得讓牠戴上口絡。
If a dog tries to eat anything on the street, the owner must put a muzzle on the dog.

到寵物店購物
buy things at the pet shop

去寵物美容院
go to the pet groomer

給…洗澡
give a bath to ~

去看獸醫；去找獸醫為寵物做健檢
visit the vet; get a check-up at the vet

清理貓砂盆
clean the litter box

玩接物遊戲
play fetch

給三隻貓洗澡真是累人。
It is exhausting to give baths to 3 cats.

和我的狗玩了三個小時的接物遊戲後，我累壞了。
I am worn out after playing fetch with my dog for 3 hours.

3

交通

TRANSPORTATION

接送（某人）
pick (somebody) up

送孩子到學校
drop one's child
off at school

走路去上班
go to work
on foot

遇到鄰居並打招呼
run into one's
neighbors and say hello

走行人穿越道過馬路
walk across the
street at a crosswalk

等候信號燈改變
wait for the light to
change

穿越行人天橋
cross / go over the
pedestrian overpass

穿越地下道
go through the
underpass

前往公車／地鐵站
move / get to the bus /
subway station

購買交通卡
buy a transit card

充值交通卡
recharge a transit card

SENTENCES TO USE

在來參加這次商務會議之前，雷伊先生必須把他的孩子送到學校。
Mr. Leigh has to drop his kid off at school before he comes to this business meeting.

茱蒂在穿越人行道前遇到了她的鄰居。
Judy ran into her neighbor before she crossed the crosswalk.

他等信號燈變綠已經一段時間了。
He has been waiting for the light to change for a while.

我小時候就討厭走行人天橋了，現在依然如此。
I hated going over the pedestrian overpass as a kid, and I still do.

我必須搭下一班火車，因為我忘了充值我的交通卡。
I had to take the next train because I forgot to recharge my transit card.

C03U1.mp3

沿著街道走
walk along the street

向路人問路
ask a passerby for directions

向人指路
show / guide the way

（往…）直走
go / walk straight (forward)

經過…
go pass ~

在…左轉
turn left at ~

在…後右轉
turn right after ~

跟著地圖指示走
follow along the map

查看抵達時間
check the arrival time

抵達目的地
arrive at the destination

在公車站排隊等候
wait in line at the bus stop

SENTENCES TO USE

一直直走，直到抵達教堂為止。
Just keep walking straight until you arrive at the church.

經過消防局，然後在行人穿越道處右轉。
Go pass the fire station and turn right at the crosswalk.

如果你沒有方向感，那就一直跟著地圖指示走吧！
If you are bad with directions, just keep following along the map!

你能查看一下你抵達的時間，好讓我去接你嗎？
Could you check your arrival time so I can go pick you up?

每當交通尖峰時我都得在公車站排隊等候。
I have to wait in line at the bus stop every rush hour.

A 你好，我想前往 ABC 飯店。你能告訴我怎麼走嗎？
▶ Hello. I'm trying to get to the ABC Hotel. Could you tell me how to get there?

B 啊，好的，稍等一下。我查看一下我手機app再告訴你。
● Ah yes, just a moment. I'll check on my phone app and let you know.

A 好的，謝謝。
▶ Okay, thanks.

B 你沿著這條路直走 200 公尺後，你會看到 XYZ 超市。然後你在那裡右轉，你會看到一條都是玩具店的巷子。走到巷子的盡頭後再左轉，會看到「東聯合車站」1 號出口。
● If you walk 200 meters straight this way, you will find the XYZ Mart. If you turn right from there, you will find the alley of the toy stores. Go to the end of that alley and turn left, and you will find Exit 1 of Eastern Union Station.

A 我應該在東聯合車站搭地鐵嗎？
▶ Should I take the subway at Eastern Union Station?

B 是的，搭前往詹姆斯鎮的地鐵1號線，在翡翠公園站下車，然後前往 5 號出口。
● Yes, take the subway Line 1 towards James Town, get off at Jade Park Station, and go to Exit 5.

從出口的反方向走約 50 公尺會有一個公車站。
● There is a bus station about 50 meters away from the opposite direction of the exit.

搭乘 123 號公車，過 4 個站後就下車。
● Take the bus number 123 and get off after 4 stations.

穿過公車站前的行人穿越道，然後往農貿市場方向步行約5分鐘。
● Cross the crosswalk in front of the bus stop and walk toward Farmsquare Market for about 5 minutes.

你到了消防局時左轉，然後走到分叉路口時，走右邊那條路。
● When you get to the fire station, turn left, and go towards the right road when the road splits.

大概走 30 多公尺，就到 ABC 飯店了。
● Walk for about 30 more meters and there will be the ABC Hotel.

A　前往那裡的路線比我想像的複雜多了。我想我還是搭計程車吧。
▶ The way there is a lot more complicated than I thought. I think I'll just take a taxi.

B　是的，那就方便多了。
● Yeah, that would be much more convenient.

只要把地點告訴司機，並使用導航系統即可。
● Just give the location to the driver and use the navigation system.

A　謝謝你的好意。
▶ Thank you for your kindness.

* carpool 也可當名詞。

開車去上班
drive one's car
to work

騎單車去…
ride a bike to ~

共乘／共享汽車
carpool;
use a car pool

搭公車／地鐵
take / ride the bus /
subway

在讀卡機上碰觸／掃描交通卡
touch / scan the transit
card to the card reader

抓住手把
hold on to a strap

玩智慧手機
play on one's smartphone

在座位上打瞌睡
doze off on the seat

讓座給孕婦／年長者
offer one's seat to a pregnant
lady / an elderly person

轉搭不同的交通工具
transfer to a different
means of transportation

坐在空曠的位子上
sit on an
empty seat

SENTENCES TO USE

傑克森通常開車上班，但他決定為了健康騎自行車。
Jackson usually drives his car to work, but he decided to ride his bike to get healthy.

我老闆安排同事們共乘汽車來上班。
My boss arranged a carpool for colleagues at work.

許多人下班後在座位上打瞌睡。
A lot of people doze off on the seat after work

因為交通堵塞，我必須轉搭地鐵。
I had to transfer to the subway because of the traffic jam.

我上公車時有位子坐，但在下一站時我把座位讓給一位年長者。
I sat on an empty seat on the bus, but I offered my seat to an elderly at the next stop.

站在走道上
stand on
the aisle

在公車上按「下車鈴」
press the 'stop' button
on the bus

下公車／下地鐵
get off the bus /
subway

穿過旋轉門出車站
come out through
the turnstile

* 出車站也可以
用 go out 表
示

經過出口出站
get out
through exit

使用／購買通勤票（卡）
buy / use a commutation
ticket / card

搭乘大眾運輸工具
use public / mass
transportation

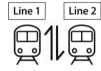

Line 1   Line 2

在…（站）轉乘 2 號線
transfer to Line
Number 2 at ~

查看公車／地鐵（路線）圖
check the bus / subway (route) map

Waaaait...

錯過一班公車／火車
miss a bus / train

查看時刻表
check the timetable

SENTENCES TO USE

巴士相當擁擠，所以米亞沒別的選擇，只能站在走道上。
The bus was so packed that Mia had no choice but to stand on the aisle.

下公車前，您必須按一下停車按鈕。
You need to press the stop button before getting off the bus.

在維多利亞車站我不可能找得到我要出站的出口。
It is impossible to find which exit I need to go out through at Victoria Station.

在平日搭乘大眾運輸工具是明智的選擇。
It is wise to use public transportation during weekdays.

如果您不想錯過巴士，查看一下時刻表吧。
Check the timetable if you don't want to miss the bus.

3 計程車

用手機叫計程車
look for a <u>taxi</u> / <u>cab</u> on the phone

用手機app叫計程車
<u>call</u> / <u>request</u> a <u>taxi</u> / <u>cab</u> with a phone app

（在路邊）招計程車
<u>grab</u> / <u>get</u> a taxi / cab

上計程車
get in (to) a <u>taxi</u> / <u>cab</u>

跟計程車司機說要去的地方
tell the driver
<u>where to go</u>
/ <u>the destination</u>

從車窗外望出去
look out the window

SENTENCES TO USE

每當天氣不好時，用手機 app 叫計程車要等很久的時間。
It takes a long time to request a taxi with a phone app whenever the weather is bad.

開始下雨了！我去招一輛計程車。
It's starting to rain! I'm just going to grab a taxi.

Ken 因為暈車，他得看向車窗外。
Ken has to look out the window due to his motion sickness.

用手機看新聞
watch the news on one's phone

用手機查看股票市場行情
check the stock market on one's phone

和計程車司機交談
have a conversation /
converse with
the taxi / cab driver

查看跳表顯示的價格
check the price on the meter

用現金／信用卡支付
pay in cash / with a card

下計程車
get out of / off the
taxi / cab

在 app 上給予這項服務評論
give / leave a review on the
app for the service

我覺得與計程車司機交談非常尷尬。
Having a conversation with the cab driver is very awkward for me.

丹尼一直在查看計程跳表上的價錢，因為他現金不夠。
Danny kept checking the price on the meter because he was short on cash.

4 駕駛

* get on the bus/train/subway

用電子鎖打開車門
open the car with the electronic key

上車
get on the car

繫上安全帶
buckle / fasten the seat belt

發動車子
start the car

調整車內後視鏡／車身後照鏡
adjust the rear-view /
side-view mirrors

切入倒車檔
shift into reverse

將車子駛出停車場
get the car out of the
parking lot

在行人穿越道前停下來
stop in front of the
crosswalk

SENTENCES TO USE

繫好安全帶再開始駕車是很重要的。
It's vital to buckle the seat belt before going out for a drive.

調整好車身後照鏡之後再切入倒車檔倒車。
Adjust the side-view mirrors before shifting into reverse.

在「注意兒童區」放慢車速
slow down at the children protection zone

在交叉路口左轉／右轉
turn <u>left</u> / <u>right</u> at the intersection

迴轉
<u>make</u> / <u>take</u> a U-turn

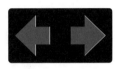

打開左轉方向燈／右轉方向燈／緊急注意燈號（閃小黃燈）
turn on the <u>left-turn</u> / <u>right-turn</u> / <u>emergency</u> signal

以倒車的方向停車
back-in park one's car

以車頭進的方向停車
head-in park one's car

進入「注意兒童區」時未減速的罰款很高。
The fine is high for not slowing down at the children protection zone.

你在右轉前務必確定沒有行人。
Always make sure there are no pedestrians before you turn right.

我母親因違規迴轉而被開了一張罰單。
My mother got a ticket for making an illegal U-turn.

將車子往路肩／路邊停靠
pull the car over to the <u>shoulder</u>
/ <u>edge of the road</u>

在收費站付過路費
pay the toll
at the tollgate

• 美國的 E-ZPass（高速公路通行）
系統就類似我們的 Electronic Toll
Collection (ETC)。

通過高速公路收費電子感應門
go through the E-ZPass at the tollgate

開上 66 號公路
drive on Route 66

開啟雨刷
turn on the wipers

轉動方向盤
steer the wheel;
turn the steering wheel

SENTENCES TO USE

如需前往飯店，請沿著 2 號公路行駛，並在經過收費站後下交流道。
To get to the hotel, drive on Route 2 and exit after the tollgate.

下雨了！請打開雨刷並按下除霧按鈕。
It's raining! Please turn on the wipers and press the demister button.

按下除霧器按鈕
press the demister button

打開車窗／天窗讓空氣流通
open the <u>window</u> / <u>sun-roof</u> to air out

到加油站加油
refuel one's car; fill (up) with gas

在自助加油站付款
pay at the gas pump

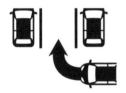

將車子停進停車格內
park the car in the parking lot

* put 也可以用
shift to 取代。

將車子打入停車檔後下車
put the car in park and get off

我忘了帶信用卡，所以車子沒辦法加油。
I forgot my credit card, so I couldn't refuel my car.

傑克喜歡在週末將他的愛車停在停車場的空位並親自洗車。
Jake loves to handwash his car parked at the vacant parking lot on the weekends.

A 既然你拿到駕照了，我們就出去上路並練習一下你的駕駛技巧吧。
▶ Since you got your driver's license, let's go out and practice your driving skills on the road.

B 這是我第一次實際上路駕駛，這樣沒問題嗎？
● It's my first-time driving on the actual road. Will it be okay?

A 別擔心，我會在副駕駛座上一直叮嚀你安全駕駛。 哈哈。
▶ Don't worry. I'll keep nagging you to drive safely in the passenger seat. Haha.

現在上車吧，繫好安全帶，並將車子發動。
▶ Now, get in the car, buckle up, and start the car.

將排檔桿推入倒車檔，將車子後退，將排檔移至 D 檔，然後踩油門並緩慢行駛。
▶ Put the gear on reverse, pull back, put the gear on drive, step on the accelerator and drive slowly.

B 唷，車子在晃，因為我煞車踩得太用力了。
● Phew, the car is shaking because I'm hitting the brakes too hard.

A 沒關係。一開始都是這樣。
▶ It's okay. it's like that at first.

輕踩煞車並保持安全距離。
▶ Step on the brakes lightly and keep a safe distance.

B 燈號變黃燈了。我得趕快通過嗎？
● The traffic light is yellow. Should I quickly pass by?

A 不，我們停車，因為我們前方的車子可能被堵住，且卡在十字路口中間。
▶ No, let's stop because the car in front of us might get stuck and block the road in the middle of the intersection.

B 我開到「注意兒童區」時要更加小心注意。
● I'm becoming more careful driving in child protection zones.

A 沒錯。你的車速必須低於 30 公里，而且你必須更加小心，因為孩子們可能會突然不知從何處冒出來。

▶ That's right. You have to drive less than 30km/h, and you have to be more careful because children can jump out of nowhere.

B 我應該在這裡迴轉嗎？

● Should I make a U-turn here?

A 是的，這個 GPS 的 app 正告訴我，在我看到左轉燈號時要迴轉，所以等到燈號出現後再迴轉吧。

▶ Yes, the GPS app is telling me to make a U-turn when I get a left turn signal, so wait until the signal comes up and make a U-turn.

B 如果我想左轉，但沒有安全的交通訊號標誌時，我應該怎麼做？

● If I want to turn left and there's an unprotected sign, what should I do?

A 查看是否有車子從另一邊駛出，當沒有車時才左轉。

▶ Check to see if the car is coming out from the other side and turn left when there is none coming.

B 哇！突然下雨了，而且霧氣也越來越濃。我的視野突然變窄了。

● Oh, it's raining all of the sudden, and it's getting foggy, too. My vision is suddenly narrowed.

A 將雨刷速度切換到最大，並打開緊急燈號（閃小黃燈），然後按下除霧按鈕。

▶ Switch the wiper to the maximum, turn on the emergency light, and press the demister button.

B 呼，我們快到了。我該把車停在哪？

● Phew ~ We're almost there. Where should I park the car?

A 你可以把車停在那邊那輛車前面。

▶ You can park in front of the car over there.

你第一次開車就表現得不錯。做得好。

▶ You did a great job for the first-time driving. Good job.

5 整理車子

洗（某人的）車
have / get one's
car washed

（自動）洗車時將車身後照鏡收起
fold the side-view mirror for
(an automatic) car wash

穿過自動洗車系統
go through an
automatic car wash

自己動手洗車
wash one's car
by hand

用一條布將車身擦乾
dry one's car with a cloth / rag

用吸塵器清理汽車內部
vacuum the interior of one's car

SENTENCES TO USE

我以前每週末都會親自動手洗車。
I used to wash my car by hand every weekend.

你應該把我車子內部吸乾淨，因為你弄得一團亂。
You should vacuum the interior of my car since you made the mess.

C03U5_1.mp3

清理地墊
clean the floor mats

擦拭儀表板
wipe off the dashboard

為輪胎打氣
pump air into a tire

添加／補充雨刷精
add / refill washer fluid / liquid

添加／更換冷卻液
add / change coolant

為車子打蠟
wax one's car

Jenna 擦拭車內的儀表板，而她丈夫用抹布把車子擦乾。
Jenna wiped off the dashboard while her husband dried the car with a rag.

我看到你的輪胎都沒氣了！請給輪胎充氣。
I can see that your tires are flat! Please pump air into your tires.

在念高中時，我的老師教過我怎麼補充雨刷精。
My teacher taught me how to refill washer fluid in high school.

將車子進廠檢驗
have / get one's car
checked / inspected

收到…的維修估價單
get / receive a repair
estimate for ~

將車子送修
have / get one's car
repaired / fixed

將引擎機油／煞車油
進行檢查／更換
have / get the engine / brake
oil checked / changed

更換車子的空氣濾清器
have one's car
air filter changed

檢查輪胎
check the tires

檢查／更換輪胎
have the tires checked / rotated

SENTENCES TO USE

Charlie收到車子的維修估價單時，差點暈倒。
Charlie almost fainted when he received the estimate for his car repair.

不管你願不願意，警示燈亮起來的話，你就得更換機油。
Whether you like it or not, you have to get the engine oil changed if the warning light is on.

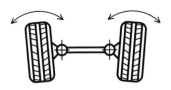

將輪胎定位
get a wheel alignment;
get the wheels aligned

（請人幫忙）更換雨刷
have the (windshield)
wipers changed

整平車身凹痕
straighten out a dent

將車身上烤漆
paint one's car;
coat one's car with paint

（請人）檢查車子的空調
have one's car air conditioner
checked

定期進行輪胎定位對安全有益。
Getting a wheel alignment regularly is good for safety.

將這凹痕整平後，我應該可以將車子烤漆。
I should be able to paint the car after straightening out this dent.

你應該找人檢查一下車子的空調，因為有異味！
You need to have your car air conditioner checked, because it smells!

4

地方

PLACES

咖啡廳

去一家咖啡廳／到咖啡廳坐坐
visit / go to a café

挑選飲料
choose drinks
/ beverages

點飲料
order drinks
/ beverages

從餐車點飲料
order drinks from a kiosk

在得來速車道點餐
order on a drive-through / drive-thru

支付飲料費用
pay for the drinks

找零
get change

* 輸入電話號碼或公
司統一編號以便日
後追查交易紀錄。

在現金收據上輸入號碼（即「打統編」）
enter in the number for a cash receipt

SENTENCES TO USE

前往考場前，我們去咖啡廳喝杯咖啡吧。
Let's go to the café and get some coffee before we head to our exam.

他支付帳單費用後忘了找零錢。
He forgot to get change after he paid for his order.

C04U1_1.mp3

輸入促銷優惠代碼
enter in a promotion code

獲得（忠實顧客的）回饋點數
earn <u>loyalty</u> / <u>frequent-customer</u> points

忘記使用／累積點數
forget to <u>use</u> /
<u>accumulate</u> points

請店員在（忠實顧客的）會員卡上蓋章
get one's <u>loyalty</u>
/ <u>frequent-customer</u> card stamped

使用電子優惠／禮物卡優待券／禮物卡
use a mobile <u>coupon</u> / <u>voucher</u>
/ <u>gift card</u>

訂購／買～外帶
buy ~ for take-out;
<u>order</u> / <u>get</u> ~ to go

付款前別忘了使用促銷優惠代碼。
Don't forget to use the promotion code before paying for the drinks.

我沒有這裡的會員卡。你要不要用你的卡來蓋章？
I don't have a loyalty card here. Would you like to get yours stamped?

我有一張生日時收到的行動禮品卡，而我打算用它來買個隨行杯。
I have a mobile gift card I got for my birthday, and I'm going to buy a tumbler with it.

將杯身套上隔熱墊
put the cup <u>holder</u>
/ <u>sleeve</u> on

拿紙巾
get napkins

將糖漿加進…
add syrup to ~

找位子坐
get <u>a table</u> / <u>seats</u>

歸還用過的馬克杯和托盤
return the used mugs
and trays

使用自助（服務）站
use the self-service
station

要一杯冰塊
get a cup of ice

SENTENCES TO USE

我們先找位子坐再點餐。
Let's get a table first before we order.

我的老師不喜歡在咖啡中加糖漿或糖。
My teacher does not like syrup or sugar added to her coffee.

你可以在自助區找些肉桂粉加到你的飲料中。
You can find some cinnamon powder to put in your drink at the self-service station.

拿到（告知可取餐的）震動鈴
get the <u>vibration bell</u> / <u>buzzer</u> / <u>pager</u>

在電子螢幕上查看（點餐）號碼
check the number on the electronic display

震動鈴響起時去拿飲料
pick up the drinks
when the pager rings

點一杯豆奶，而非一般鮮奶
order soy milk instead
of regular milk; replace
regular milk with soy milk

點一杯低脂鮮奶，而非一般鮮奶
order low-fat milk instead of regular milk;
replace regular milk with low-fat milk

點一杯無咖啡因的飲料
order a decaffeinated drink;
order decaff

她每次點餐都會點豆奶而非一般牛奶，因為她有乳糖不耐受症。
She replaces regular milk with soy milk in all her orders, because she is lactose intolerant.

我傍晚都會點一杯無咖啡因低脂拿鐵。
I always order decaff low-fat latte in the evening.

A　你好，可以點餐嗎？
　　▶ Hello. Can I order, please?

B　歡迎光臨。內用還是外帶？
　　● Welcome. For here, or to go?

A　內用。我想要一杯淡一點的熱美式咖啡和一杯冰拿鐵，謝謝。
　　▶ For here. I would like a weak hot americano and an iced latte, please.

　　還有一個烤箱烘焙的奶油起司貝果和一塊起司蛋糕。
　　● And one oven-baked cream cheese bagel and a piece of cheesecake, too.

B　好的，熱美式和冰拿鐵的大小呢？
　　● Okay, what size would you like for your hot americano and iced latte?

A　熱美式要小杯的，拿鐵要中杯的，謝謝。
　　▶ Small size for the americano and a medium for the latte, please.

B　我們咖啡廳的顧客將使用馬克杯裝飲料，時間限制為四小時。
　　● Customers using our café will be served drinks in mugs and the usage time is limited to 4 hours.

　　這樣可以嗎？
　　● Would that be all right?

A　那很好。能換低脂牛奶並在上面加點鮮奶油嗎？
　　▶ That's perfect. Could you replace the milk for low-fat milk and add whipping cream on top?

B　鮮奶油要另加一美元，可以嗎？
　　● Whipping cream is an extra dollar, is that okay?

A　好的。這是我的卡。
　　▶ That's good. Here is my card.

B　哦不，這張卡有點問題。能換一張卡支付嗎？
　　● Oh no, this card has an error. Could you pay with another card?

A　好的，那我要使用我的行動禮品卡。
▶ Oh, then I will use my mobile gift card.

B　當然可以。您已支付12美元。
● Sure. 12 dollars was charged.

還有38美元的餘額可供日後使用。
● 38 dollars is left in the balance for later use.

您需要現金收據嗎？
● Would you like a cash receipt?

A　是的，我用我的手機號碼。
▶ Yes, I'll use my phone number.

B　謝謝。這是您的振動鈴，響鈴後您可以到取餐區拿取您的飲料。
● Thank you. Here is your vibration bell, and you can come get your drinks at the pick-up zone once it buzzes.

您還需要什麼嗎？
● Do you need anything else?

A　這杯美式咖啡要加兩顆糖漿，也請給我一些餐巾。
▶ Could you add 2 pumps of syrup for the americano, and give me some napkins?

B　糖漿和餐巾在那邊的自助服務區。
● Syrup and napkins are at the self-service station over there.

A　非常感謝。
▶ Thank you very much.

COFFE
LATTE
MOCHA
ESPRESSO
MACCIATO　　LEMONADE
CAPPUCCINO　　　　TEA

2 點餐時的狀況

不小心點了…而沒點到…
order ~ instead of ...
by mistake

拿的是別人的飲料／訂餐
get someone else's <u>drink</u> / <u>order</u>

拿的不是自己點的飲料／訂的餐點（訂餐弄錯）
get a different drink than one ordered;
mix up drinks; have an order mix-up

取消支付
cancel payment

取得部分退款
get a partial refund

用錯付款方式；付錯款
make a wrong
payment

用了一張無效的／已逾期的卡片
use an <u>invalid</u> / <u>expired</u> card

SENTENCES TO USE

哦不，我不小心點了冰茶，沒點到熱茶。
Oh no, I ordered iced tea instead of hot tea by mistake.

Liam 因為他的訂餐被弄錯了而必須與咖啡店經理起爭執。
Liam had to argue with the cafe manager because of his order mix-up.

Emma 因為蛋糕賣光了而取得部分退款。
Emma got a partial refund for the sold out piece of cake.

刷卡被拒
card service unavailable

信用卡無法讀取／卡片沒過
be unable to <u>read</u> / <u>use</u> a credit card;
one's card doesn't go through

更改支付方式
change payment
method

因為前一杯飲料不好喝／壞了而再買／再點一杯
<u>buy</u> / <u>order</u> another drink because the
previous drink <u>didn't taste good</u> / <u>was bad</u>

訂餐被遺漏了
an order is <u>left out</u> / <u>missing</u>

因自助點餐機故障無法點餐
be unable to order due to an error in the kiosk

昨天我的卡片沒過，也許是已經過期了。
My card did not go through yesterday, maybe it's expired.

昨天那間咖啡廳因自助點餐機故障只能收現金。
That cafe was accepting only cash yesterday due to an error in the kiosk.

去便利商店
go to a convenience store

買急救箱
buy a first-aid kit

查看…的有效日期
check the expiration
date of ~

用微波爐將速食加熱
heat up instant food in the
microwave

尋找折扣商品
look for a
discounted product

買標準垃圾袋
buy a standard
garbage bag

SENTENCES TO USE

你在付款前應檢查折扣商品的有效日期。
You should check the expiration date of the discounted products before paying.

我將我的魚餅串在微波爐中加熱後再食用。
I heat up my fish cake skewers in the microwave before eating them.

* 在美國部分的州，便利
  商店有賣彩券，如果是
  在台灣，就只能去彩券
  行（lottery retailer）買
  了。

到便利商店買彩券
**buy a lottery ticket
at a convenience store**

查看身分證以確認年齡
check one's ID for one's age

在店裡吃東西
**eat one's food
at the store**

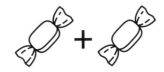

購買「買1送1」的東西
**buy a one-plus-one product;
buy one-get-one free**

選購4瓶以上有折扣優惠的啤酒
**choose a beer with a discount on
purchases of more than four cans**

到便利商店買一張彩券中獎的機會有多大？
What are the chances of buying a single lottery ticket at a convenience store and winning?

當我試著要買香煙時，一名計時的店員查看了我的身份證。
A part-timer checked my ID when I tried to buy cigarettes.

你的杯裝泡麵要在店內吃還是帶回家吃？
Are you going to eat cup noodles at the store or take them home?

C04U4.mp3

順道去一家書店
stop by a
bookstore

看看／找尋暢銷書
<u>check out</u> / <u>look for</u>
the bestseller

查詢一本書的位置
search the location
of a book

做書籍的比較
compare
books

選了一本書
choose a
book

隨便翻翻一本書／雜誌
<u>thumb</u> / <u>leaf</u>
through <u>a magazine</u>
/ <u>book</u>

出示優惠券
<u>show</u> / <u>give</u> a
discount coupon

領取一本線上預購的書
pick up a book
paid online

去一家二手書店看看
go to a
<u>secondhand</u> / <u>used</u>
bookstore

把舊書賣給二手書店
sell one's used books
to the secondhand
bookstore

在網路書店買了／
訂購一本書
<u>buy</u> / <u>order</u> a book at
an online bookstore

買／訂購電子書
<u>buy</u> / <u>order</u>
an eBook

將書運送至某人住家／公司
have books
delivered to one's
<u>house</u> / <u>company</u>

SENTENCES TO USE

Mia 順道去書店查看一下她的書是否上了暢銷榜。
Mia stopped by the bookstore to check if her book is on the bestseller list.

不好意思，能幫我找一下這本書的位置嗎？
Excuse me, could you help me look for the location of this book?

我總是在買書之前先瀏覽一章。
I always leaf through a chapter of a book before buying it.

他從不把他用過的書賣給二手書店。
He never sells his used books to the secondhand bookstore.

Jason 在病假期間無法外出時，上網購買電子書。
Jason bought eBooks online when he was on sick leave and couldn't leave his house.

5 閒聊

C04U5.mp3

相互問候
exchange greetings

聊聊天，閒聊一下
have a chat

打聽…（某人）的消息
inquire after ~

向…（某人）問候
say hello to ~; send one's regards to ~

* 這句話主要用於藉由某人向另一人問候

聊聊目前的狀況
talk / chat about current situation

聊聊目前的熱門話題
talk / chat about the hot topic

炫耀…
brag / show off about / on ~

* '得到稱讚'
get compliment on

讚美…（某物或事）
compliment about / on ~

對於…感到遺憾
regret about / on ~

背後說某人壞話
talk behind one's back

說再見／道別
say goodbye / farewell

SENTENCES TO USE

我每天早上都會和咖啡館經理互相打招呼。
I exchange greetings with the cafe manager every morning.

我們何不來聊聊目前的熱門話題？
Why don't we have a chat about the current hot topic?

請替我向你媽媽問好。
Please send my regards to your mother for me.

每次我外出時，人們總是讚美我的彩色陽傘。
I always get compliments on my colorful parasol whenever I go out.

我不喜歡背地裡說人壞話，但我真的很討厭我妹妹炫耀她的新車。
I don't like talking behind anybody's back but I really hate it when my sister brags about her new car.

A　嗨，潔米！你好嗎？好久不見！
▶ Hello Jaime! How are you? It's been a long time!

B　嘿，邁克。真是好久不見！
● Hey, Michael. It's been ages!

我們多久沒見了？
● How long has it been?

A　自從在你大畢業典禮上見過面之後，已經過了將近兩年了。
▶ It's been almost 2 years since I saw you at your college graduation.

你看起來都沒變耶。
▶ You look the same now and then.

B　不過你瘦了很多。當初臉圓圓的，現在變得修長且英俊。
● But you lost a lot of weight. The one who had a plump face is now very slim and handsome.

A　噢，別客氣。我認為是我開始努力運動以來，讓一些事情改變了。
▶ Oh, please. I guess some things have changed since I've been working out a lot.

B　你看起來瘦了許多，且容光煥發。
● You look much slimmer and splendid.

你最近過得如何？
● How are things going for you?

A　我換工作後忙著適應新公司並讓自己上手。
▶ I was busy settling down in my new company after I changed jobs.

我目前在海外的銷售部門工作，所以經常到很多國家出差。
▶ I'm currently working in an overseas sales department, so I travel to a lot of countries.

C04U5_PU.mp3

適應時差和新環境並不容易，但我喜歡遇見各式各樣的人，並體驗新的文化。

▶ It's hard to adjust to the time difference and new environment, but I'm enjoying meeting various people and experiencing new cultures.

那麼你呢？

▶ How about you?

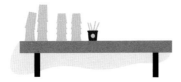

B 我在第一家公司做得還不錯，最近換到一家娛樂事業代理商。

● I was doing okay at my first company, and recently moved to an entertainment agency.

雖然我獲得不錯的待遇，不過在上一份工作中遇到一些人際間相處的困難。

● I received a good offer while having a hard time with people at my previous job.

A 為什麼，在那家公司發生了什麼事？畢竟那是你夢想的工作。

▶ Why, what happened at that company? It was your dream to work there.

B 工作氛圍很好，但其中一位老闆經常刁難我。

● The work atmosphere was great but one of the bosses kept tormenting me.

事情不是我的錯，但他卻把事情公開說的好像都是我的錯才會出問題。

● It was not my fault, but he reported it as if I made a mistake and caused the issue.

而不久前，我策劃的專案想法被評為極佳的點子，但他抄襲了我的想法，以他的名義上傳了那項專案，奪走原本我會獲得的獎項。

● And not long ago, the project idea I planned was chosen to be the superb idea, but he copied it and uploaded the project under his name to take away the award I was going to receive.

我辭職後換過幾份工作，因為我氣炸了。

● I quit and moved jobs because I was furious.

A 哇！聽起來像是電視劇的情節！你當時一定非常沮喪吧。

▶ Wow! That sounds like drama material! You must have been so frustrated.

那麼新公司如何呢？

▶ How about your new workplace?

B 這個地方就像個天堂。

● This place is like heaven.

工作氣氛佳，且我覺得如果我能遇到很多名人，有助於我在職場中站穩腳步，且我會努力工作。

● The atmosphere is great and I think it will help me build a career if I meet many celebrities and work hard.

A 這真是好消息。那麼你的感情世界呢？

▶ Good to hear! How about your love business?

B 嗯，我單身已經一段時間了。

● Hmm, I have been single for a while.

A 為什麼？你都沒有認識任何人嗎？

● Why? Do you know anyone?

B 事實上，是有的！

▶ As a matter of fact, I do!

A 對於相親你有什麼感覺？

▶ How do you feel about a blind date?

我有一位親密的同事，也許你們可以相處得很好。

▶ I have a close colleague who would get along with you.

B　相親嗎？如果你介紹他給我，他應該會是可靠的人，所以我完全可以接受！

　　● A blind date? If you are introducing him to me, he should be a reliable man, so I am totally in!

A　好的，太棒了。那我安排一下時間後通知你。

　　▶ Okay, awesome. Then I will arrange the schedule and let you know.

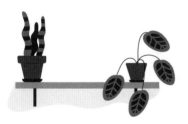

CHAPTER

5

學校生活

SCHOOL LIFE

學校生活

經過行人穿越道時和教官打招呼
<u>greet</u> / <u>say hello to</u> the guard at the crosswalk

傳訊息給朋友
text (with) friends

把東西塞進置物櫃
<u>put</u> / <u>shove</u> one's stuff in one's locker

在學校操場上踢足球
play soccer in the schoolyard

整理桌子
clean (up) one's desk

跟老師打招呼
<u>greet</u> / <u>bow to</u> / <u>say hello to</u> the teacher

SENTENCES TO USE

大多數男孩喜歡在學校操場踢足球。
Most of the boys like to play soccer in the schoolyard.

我通常會把我的東西塞進櫃子裡，並在上課前整理我的書桌。
I usually shove my stuff in the locker and clean my desk before class.

決定大掃除的分配工作
decide on <u>clean-up</u> / <u>cleaning</u> duty

決定和誰同一張桌子
decide on a seating partner

被老師斥責
get a scolding from one's teacher;
<u>be</u> / <u>get</u> scolded by one's teacher

在課堂上打瞌睡
<u>doze</u> / <u>nod</u> off
in class

在筆記本上亂畫
<u>scribble</u> / <u>doodle</u> on one's notebook

整理班級公佈欄
organize one's class bulletin board

每個星期由不同的人擔任清潔工作的值日生。
People on cleaning duty change every week.

學生在課堂上打瞌睡時會被老師責罵。
Students get scolded by their teacher when they doze off in class.

我過去常和我朋友一起整理班級公佈欄。
I used to organize the class bulletin board with my friend.

A 你聽說了嗎？我們班的班長將獲頒教育部長獎了。
▶ Did you hear? Our class president is getting the Minister of Education Award.

B 我們班長？你指的是山姆嗎？他真是棒。他為什麼可以得獎？
● Our class president? Are you talking about Sam? Good for him. What for?

A 是的，他參加一場創意構思的比賽，要提出如何創造更有助益以及更有意義的校園生活，而他贏得了這項大獎。
▶ Yes, he entered an idea contest to come up with ways to create more helpful and meaningful school life and he won the grand prize.

B 直到去年，他還因不斷地與其他學生打架以及翹課而被停學。
● Until last year, he was suspended for constantly fighting with other students and skipping classes.

這一年來有了什麼改變嗎？
● What changed in a year?

A 去年他因長期無故缺課而幾乎面臨被退學，但我們的班導師說服他再努力試試。
▶ He almost got expelled last year for extended unexcused absences, but our class teacher persuaded him to give one more try.

他建議山姆參加書友會。
▶ He recommended Sam to join the book club.

B 山姆在書友會裡非常努力用功。
● Sam worked really hard in that book club.

我聽說他就是在學校活動中主辦書本理解測驗的人，而這活動非常成功。真是太棒了！
● I heard that he was the one who organized the book quiz event at the school event which turned out super successful. That's amazing!

A 沒錯，顯然自從他讀過很多書之後，他的生活態度有所改變了。
▶ Yup, apparently his attitude toward his life has changed since he read a lot of books.

過去他常對媽媽謊稱他去補習數學，實際上卻跑去網咖打電動。
▶ He used to lie to his mom that he was going to math academy and went to an Internet cafe to play games instead.

但現在他不會再躲避課後課程或補習班，且會前往K書中心唸書後再回家。
▶ But now he does not skip any after-school classes or academy, and studies at a study cafe before heading home.

B 他有發生什麼事嗎？他已經長大了。
● What happened to him? He has grown up.

A 我聽說山姆明年要角逐學生會會長。
▶ I heard Sam is running for school president next year.

我最好得反省自己了，且從現在開始更加努力用功。
▶ I better reflect on myself and study harder from now on.

C05U2.mp3

去小吃攤
go to the <u>kiosk</u>
/ <u>snack bar</u>

趴在桌上小睡一下
lie down on
one's desk for a nap

找朋友一起上廁所
go to the toilet with
one's friend

跟朋友聊天
<u>chat</u> / <u>have a chat</u>
with one's friend

跟朋友一起享用小吃
<u>have</u> / <u>eat</u> a snack
with one's friend

去教師休息室
go to the teacher's
lounge

去保健室
go to the <u>nurse's office</u>
/ <u>school infirmary</u>

清理／整理板子
<u>clean</u> / <u>organize</u>
the board

擦板子
erase the board

* PE 是指 physical education。

換穿體育服
change into <u>gym</u>
/ <u>PE</u> clothes

下課鈴聲響起
a recess bell rings;
a bell rings for recess

SENTENCES TO USE

湯姆在下課時趴在他的桌上小睡一會兒。
Tom lies down on his desk for a short nap during recess.

我一直很好奇為什麼女生們都會找朋友一起去上洗手間。
I always wondered why girls go to the toilet with their friends.

她過去曾經在去這家小販攤的路上和朋友聊天。
She used to chat with her friend on the way to the kiosk.

我們的班長總是在下課鐘響起時擦黑板,為下一節課做準備。
Our class president always erases the board for the next class when the recess bell rings.

學生們必須換上學校體育課的運動服。
Students have to change into school gym clothes for PE class.

3 課堂上

C05U3.mp3

把課本打開
open one's textbook

專心上課
concentrate on the study

*強調「用心上課」
聆聽某位老師的課
listen to one's teacher's class

去上某一位老師的課
take one's teacher's class

*強調「去上課」
這件事

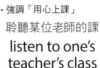

舉手問問題
raise one's hand to ask a question

回答老師的問題
answer the teacher's question

被抓到在課堂上和同學聊天
get caught chatting with one's friend in class

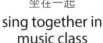

上音樂課時
坐在一起
sing together in music class

上美術課時畫畫
paint / draw in art class

*實驗。

上自然科學課時做實驗
(do an) experiment in science class

上課時發呆
space / zone out during class

翹課，逃學
play hooky; skip class

考試作弊
cheat on one's exam / test

SENTENCES TO USE

在課堂上總是有一位模範生會舉手回答所有問題。
There is always a model student to raise his/her hand in class and answer all the questions.

他在課堂上被抓到在課本上畫畫。
He got caught drawing on his textbook in class.

我懷念在學生時代時，經常在溫暖的春風中發呆的時光。
I miss my time at school when I used to space out under the warm spring breeze.

我妹妹習慣翹課並在校外吃拉麵。
My younger sister had a habit of playing hooky and eating ramen outside school.

我的朋友總是考試作弊，所以我檢舉她。
My friend always cheats on her test, so I told on her.

C05U4.mp3

競選學生會會長
run for school
president

競選班長
run for class
president

舉辦運動會
hold a <u>sports</u> /
<u>field</u> day

辦一堂觀摩教學課
<u>have</u> / <u>hold</u> an
open class

去校外野餐
go on a class
picnic

（坐遊覽車）去遠足
go on a school <u>trip</u>
/ <u>excursion</u>

退出學生社團
<u>withdraw</u>
<u>drop out</u> /
from a club

加入學生社團
join <u>a club</u>
/ <u>an after-school club</u>

為校園慶祝活動做準備
prepare for the
school festival

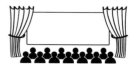

缺席…
be absent
from ~

提早下課，提早離校
leave school early;
take an early leave

轉學至另一所學校
／從另一所學校轉來
transfer <u>to</u> / <u>from</u> a
different school

被學校停學
<u>be</u> / <u>get</u>
suspended from
school

被學校退學
<u>be</u> / <u>get</u>
expelled
from
school

SENTENCES TO USE

我在學生時代為了好玩參選班長。

I ran for class president for fun when I was a student.

小學時，我父母總是會來參加運動會。
My parents always came to the sports day in my elementary school.

我曾經參加美術社，但後來退出後加入攝影社。
I used to be in an art club but I dropped out from that club to join a photography club.

他因為慢性病而經常上課缺席。
He was absent from school frequently due to chronic illness.

Michael 在一次校外旅行時帶酒而遭到停學。
Michael got suspended from school after he brought alcohol on a school trip.

C05U5.mp3

清理教室
clean one's
classroom

跟朋友一起放學回家
come / return home
from school with friends

搭上校車
get on the
school bus

去操場玩
go to the
playground

上課後班
take an
after-school class

搭乘學校巴士
take / ride an
academy bus

去上〇〇補習班
go to academy for
OO / OO academy

去K書中心
go to / visit
a study cafe

去朋友家裡玩
go to / visit one's
friend's house

跟朋友在家玩樂
hang out with
one's friend
at home

到網咖打電動
go to an Internet / a PC
cafe to play games

做功課
do one's homework

SENTENCES TO USE

我從未有機會和朋友一起放學回家，因為我忙著上英語補習班。
I never had the chance to come home from school with friends, because I was busy getting to English academy.

過去，我常常不去上課後班，而是翹課去操場和朋友玩耍。
I used to skip the after-school class to go to the playground and play with my friends.

今天校車提早到達，所以山姆無法去朋友家。
The school bus arrived early today, so Sam could not go to his friend's house.

我媽媽以前常去一家當地網咖找我哥哥。
My mother used to go to a local Internet cafe to search for my older brother.

我的一位朋友總是堅持在搭校車前做她的家庭作業。
One of my friends always insisted on doing her homework before getting on the school bus.

C05U6.mp3

去學校上班
go to work
at school

出席學校朝會
<u>attend</u> / <u>go to a</u>
morning assembly

查看教室是否乾淨整潔
check the
cleanliness of the
classroom

準備教學課綱
<u>prepare</u> / <u>make</u>
a <u>teaching</u> / <u>lesson</u> plan

授課
conduct
one's class

頒發個獎給學生
give an award to
a student; award
a student

訓斥搗蛋的學生
discipline
a troubled
student

出考題
make exam
questions

監考
supervise an
examination

記錄學生的成績
<u>keep</u> / <u>make</u>
/ <u>write up</u> a
student record

與學生家長面談
consult one's
student's parents

與令人頭痛
／惹麻煩的學生商談
<u>consult</u> / <u>have a</u>
<u>consultation with</u> a
<u>troubled</u> / <u>worried</u> student

發給學生校外遠足同意書
<u>distribute</u> / <u>hand out</u>
school excursion
consent forms to the
students

SENTENCES TO USE

所有老師每個週一都必須參加朝會。
All teachers have to attend a morning assembly every Monday.

準備教學課綱對老師們來說並不容易。
Preparing a teaching plan is not an easy thing for teachers.

老師在授課時回答學生們的問題。
A teacher answers the students' questions while conducting his class.

與令人頭痛的學生之家長商談學生在校表現紀錄的重要性，是老師工作的一部分。
Consulting troubled student's parents about the importance of a student record is part of teacher's job.

數學老師今年將期中考題設計得特別難。
The math teacher made midterm exam questions especially hard this year.

7 大學生活

C05U7_1.mp3

申請大學入學
apply for <u>college</u> / <u>university</u>

收到學校的入學通知書
receive / <u>get</u> an admission letter / <u>a letter of admission</u>

支付學雜費
pay for one's tuition

獲得學貸
<u>take out</u> / <u>receive</u> a student loan

主修…
major in ~

報名選修課程
<u>register</u> / <u>sign up</u> for courses; enroll in classes

參加新生訓練會（OT）
participate in / experience / <u>go through</u> an OT (= orientation)

上課
take a class

參加線上課程
take an online class

加入／報名參加學生會
<u>join</u> / <u>sign up for</u> a student council

修習…的雙主修
double-major in ~

SENTENCES TO USE

我很開心申請大學並收到錄取通知書。
I was so excited to apply for college and get the letter of admission.

請不要忘記在截止日期前繳交學費。
Please don't forget to pay for your tuition by the deadline.

Lucas忘記準時選課，因此他這一年的課程表被打亂了。
Lucas forgot to sign up for courses on time so his class schedule is destroyed for the year.

Judy加入學生會而增加了更多工作負擔。
Judy added more workload by joining the student council.

她正在修習生物學和藝術史的雙主修。
She is double-majoring in biology and art history.

獲得獎學金
get / receive
a scholarship

被留校查看；被學校記警告
get placed under academic
probation; receive a school warning

加入一場讀書會
participate in / join
a study group

參加社團活動
participate in / join
a club activity

參加（大學的）兄弟會
／女子聯誼會（等社交俱樂部）
join a fraternity /
sorority

進行小組專案計畫
do a group
project

與…（某人）
在圖書館唸書
study in the library
with ~

獨自在…唸書
study alone at ~

為…（某個科目）
臨時抱佛腳
cram for ~;
hit the books;
last-minute study for ~

參加期中／期末考
take a midterm /
final exam

SENTENCES TO USE

她在被留校查看之後失去了獎學金。
She lost her scholarship after getting placed under academic probation.

新學期開始時，他加入了羽球社和跳傘社團。
He joined a badminton club and a skydiving club when the new semester started.

多數大學生都對於加入兄弟會或女子聯誼會抱有幻想。
Most university students have a fantasy about joining a fraternity or a sorority.

我在進行小組專案時遇到有些人想「搭便車」的問題。
I had issues with doing group projects because of free riders.

過去我常在期中考前臨時抱佛腳，但現在不再這樣了。
I used to cram for my midterms, but I don't do it anymore.

從…（某地）通勤前來
commute from ~

住宿舍
live in a dormitory

獨自謀生
make one's own living; live by oneself

兼差打工
work at a part-time
job; work part-time

擔任家教工作
give private
lessons

成為大學情侶
become a college couple
/ college sweethearts

上課遲到
be late
for class

請假沒來上課
apply for a leave
of absence
(from college)

申請返校上課
apply to go back
to college

舉辦畢業展
hold / have a graduation
exhibition

SENTENCES TO USE

她每天從這個城鎮郊區通勤來上課。
She is commuting from the outskirts of the town to take classes.

Sammy入伍前住了一個學期的學生宿舍。
Sammy lived in a dormitory for one semester before going off to serve in the army.

過去我曾經兼差當家教，賺點生活費。
I used to give private lessons and work part-time to earn living expenses.

我在學生時代時和校園相親認識的女生成為了大學情侶。
I became a college couple with the girl I had a blind date with on campus.

我們舉辦了一場攝影系的畢業展，且辦得相當成功。
We held a graduation exhibition for our photography major and it was a great success.

A 吉娜，我錄取 NIT 理工學院生物科技系了！
▶ Gena, I got accepted to the Department of Biotechnology at NIT!

B 哇！恭喜你。你確實非常努力準備這次的入學重考。
● Wow! Congratulations. You studied really hard to retake the entrance exam.

NIT 理工學院是你心儀大學名單中的首選。
● NIT University was on the top of your list of your desired universities.

A 謝謝你。
▶ Thank you.

昨天我參加了迎新活動，教授們似乎都很親切，學長姐們也很照顧我，整個氣氛都非常棒。
▶ I went to the orientation yesterday, and the professors seemed kind, the senior students took good care of me and the whole atmosphere was great.

我真的很期待下週去詹姆斯城參加聚會活動。
▶ I'm really looking forward to going to James Town for the get-together next week.

B 這聽起來還不錯。
● That sounds great.

聽起來你現在開始真正踏入大學生活了。
● Sounds like you're starting your real college life now.

放輕鬆，還不必急著選課。
● Take it easy and don't get greedy about registering for classes.

我還是大一新生時，第一個學期登記選了 24 個學分，雖然我努力修學分，但幾乎快被逼死了。
● I registered 24 credits for my first semester as a freshman and I almost died trying to manage my grades.

幸好，我沒有被列入學業審查，因為我兩次期末考都很糟糕，拿到兩個不及格。
● Luckily, I didn't get placed under academic probation, because I got two Fs after messing up two finals.

A 我想在大學的第一年積極參與社團活動，並體驗大學情侶的生活，所以在選課上我得放輕鬆一點。

▶ I want to be active in club activities and experience being a college couple as a freshman, so I gotta go easy on taking classes.

大學的第一年過後，我打算到美國申請交換學生一年，然後休學去服兵役，再回來努力用功念書。

▶ After my first year in college, I'm going to apply to be an exchange student to the U.S. for a year, take a leave of absence for military service and come back and work hard.

B 你對未來已經有明確的計劃！你真棒！

● You have all your plans for the future! Good for you.

我考慮在大學休學後再次參加大學入學考試。

● I am thinking about taking the college entrance exam again after dropping out of college.

A 為什麼？有什麼事嗎？

▶ Why, what happened?

B 我覺得我目前的主修科系不太適合我。

● I don't think my major is a good fit for me.

我擔心畢業後我能否在這個專業領域有良好的表現。

● I'm worried if I can do well working in this area of expertise after graduation.

A 真的嗎？那真是進退兩難了。

▶ Really? That's a dilemma.

我的意見是，最好先請假一段時間，且在你得知另一場入學考試的結果之後再做決定，以免你日後可能又會改變心意。

▶ To give you my opinion, it would be better to take a leave of absence and decide after looking at your results for another entrance exam just in case you change your mind later on.

B 是的，這似乎是最好的選擇。謝謝。

● Yeah, that seems like the best option. Thanks.

拍畢業照
take graduation album photos

盛裝打扮
dress oneself up

戴上畢業帽（學士帽或碩士帽）
wear a graduation cap

穿上畢業袍（學士袍或碩士袍）
wear a graduation gown

邀請家人／親戚來參加某人的畢業典禮
invite one's <u>family</u> /
<u>relatives</u> to one's graduation
ceremony

參加某人的畢業典禮
<u>attend</u> / <u>participate in</u> / <u>go to</u>
one's graduation ceremony

SENTENCES TO USE

我很高興我所有家人都來參加我的畢業典禮。
I was very happy that my whole family attended my graduation ceremony.

她是她家第一位穿上畢業袍以及戴上畢業帽的人。
She was the first one to wear a graduation gown and cap in her family.

C05U8.mp3

取得學位證書
<u>get</u> / <u>receive</u> a diploma

扔掉學士帽
throw one's graduation cap

跟同學一起拍畢業照
take graduation photos with one's classmates

聆聽（學生代表的）告別致詞
listen to the valedictorian speech

聆聽訓導主任／校長的祝賀詞
listen to the <u>dean's</u> / <u>president's</u> congratulatory speech

我們努力用功才能夠拿到這張學位證書！
We worked so hard to get this diploma!

所有人一起來拍一張將畢業帽拋向空中的照片。
Everyone takes a photo of throwing their graduation caps in the air.

聽訓導主任的賀辭真是無聊。
Listening to the dean's congratulatory speech was a drag.

CHAPTER

6

職場生活

LIFE AT WORK

求職／找工作
<u>look</u> / <u>search</u> for a job
(position); seek employment

撰寫履歷／求職信
write <u>a resume</u>
/ <u>an application</u>

撰寫求職信
write <u>a self-introduction letter</u>
/ <u>a cover letter</u>

進行工作性向測驗
<u>conduct</u> / <u>get</u> a job
aptitude test

向教授要一封推薦信
ask the professor for a letter of
<u>recommendation</u> / <u>reference</u> / <u>referral</u>

SENTENCES TO USE

我和我的朋友開始尋找實習工作。
My friends and I started looking for jobs as an intern.

我已寄出一大堆應徵信函和求職信給許多家公司，但沒有一家公司打電話給我。
I sent tons of applications and cover letters to multiple companies, but none called me back.

Sophia 參加一項工作性向測驗，且她馬上就知道這家公司不太適合她。
Sophia got a job aptitude test and she knew right away that the company was not a good fit for her.

我需要三位不同教授的推薦信。
I need three letters of recommendation from three different professors.

C06U1.mp3

應徵某家公司
apply to a company

等候工作面試
wait for a job interview

參加面試
have / go to an
interview

收到錄取／未錄取的通知（信）
receive / get a notification (letter) of
acceptance / rejection

收到備取通知
receive a waiting notice;
get wait-listed

我在等待工作面試時非常緊張。
I was very nervous waiting for a job interview.

應徵後被列入備取名單的感覺不是很好。
It's not a good feeling to get wait-listed for a job position.

A 感謝您應徵本公司。
▶ Thank you for applying to our company.

我們已經看過您的履歷和求職信。
▶ We have gone through your resume and cover letter.

您似乎在求學時有豐富的實習經驗，同時也有各種校外活動的經驗。
▶ You seem to have a lot of experience in field training, as well as various outside activities while attending school.

B 是的，我在大學擔任學生會會長期間，經歷過許多與學系相關的行政工作。
● Yes, I experienced a lot of administrative work related to the department while I was student body president of the university.

在我的教授指導下，我在執行各種專案時一直努力與企業主管保持順暢的溝通。
● And I worked hard for smooth communication with corporate officials while working on various projects under my professor.

A 職業性向測驗也顯示非常好的結果。
▶ The job aptitude test also showed very good results.

我們對一件事很好奇，那就是您在上一份工作僅做了短短 5 個月就離開了。您能告訴我們原因嗎？
▶ One thing we are curious about is that you left your previous workplace after working for a short 5 month. Could you tell us the reason?

B 上一份工作的辦公室氣氛以及同事們都很好，但我的工作內容無法讓我做到最佳的發揮。
● The atmosphere of the previous office and colleagues were great, but my job description was not something I could do best.

我決定盡快換一份工作，以免為時已晚，因為在一個我能充分發揮自己能力的職位上工作，可能對公司有幫助且可以讓我更有動力。

● I decided to move on to a different job quickly before it was too late, because working in a position where I perform best with my abilities to the fullest might help this company and motivate me.

A 嗯，好的，我明白了。如果你加入我們公司，你有何計畫呢？

▶ Oh, yes, I see. What do you plan to do if you join our company?

B 因為我在念大學時參加過各種活動，並在此類專案計畫中結識了多位公司代表，我了解自己善於人際關係的管理，且我擁有不錯的溝通能力。

● As I participated in various activities in college and met many company representatives in such projects, I learned that I am good at managing interpersonal relationships and have excellent communication skills.

如果我有機會加入貴公司，我想要待在銷售支援團隊工作，那麼我就能夠充分展現我的能力。

● If I get the chance to join your company, I would like to work in the sales support team so that I can show my abilities to the fullest.

A 感謝你的回答。

▶ Thank you for your answer.

我們將在本週完成所有人員的面試，並於下週讓你知道結果。感謝您的辛勞。

▶ We will finish up the interview by this week and let you know the result next week. Thank you for your effort.

加入某公司
join / enter
a company / firm

去上班
go to work
/ the office; report
for duty

查看當日／每日工作行程
check the schedule for
the day / one's daily
schedule

擔任實習生
do an internship;
become an intern

接受新進人員的訓練
receive / get
training for new
employees

進行實地培訓
conduct field
training

聆聽／遵從老闆的指示
listen to / follow one's
boss's instructions

向老闆報告
report to
one's boss

做筆記
take notes
/ a memo

拿到加班費
get overtime pay;
get paid overtime

領取員工識別證
get an employee card
/ badge reissued

透過公司通訊軟體傳送訊息
send a message through
the company messenger

SENTENCES TO USE

Oliver期待進入一家公司並展開其新進人員培訓。
Oliver is looking forward to entering a company and starting his training as a new employee.

他習慣和主管核對他的每日工作行程。
He has a habit of checking his daily schedule with his supervisor.

William相當嚴謹地查看工作行程以及遵循主管指示
William is very strict on checking schedules and following his supervisor's instructions.

若您有訊息要留給Chris先生的話，我可以先記下來。
I can take a memo if you have a message for Mr. Chris.

Holly曾經透過公司通訊軟體發送出令人尷尬的私人訊息。
Holly once sent an embarrassing private message through the company messenger.

接電話
answer the phone

轉接電話
transfer a phone call

掛電話
hang up the phone

整理資料／檔案
organize one's
material / file

做文書工作
complete / write up
a document (file);
do paperwork

影印一些…
make some
copies of ~

在文件上蓋章
stamp the
document

提交文件
submit the
document

獲得老闆的認可
obtain / get approval from the
boss; get a sanction from the boss

用傳真機／電子郵件傳送文件
send a document
by fax / e-mail

銷毀文件
shred a
document

SENTENCES TO USE

對方還在講電話時就把電話掛斷是很不禮貌的。
It is rude to hang up the phone when someone is talking on the line.

請整理好你的文件，不然會變得一團亂（無法掌控）。
Please organize your files before things get out of hand.

我辭職了，因為我所做的事情就只是複印文件以及蓋章。
I quit my job because all I did was making copies of documents and stamping them.

別忘了要取得老闆的批准才能發送傳真。
Don't forget to get approval from the boss before you send the fax.

當我還是一名新進員工時，我不小心將重要文件銷毀了。
When I was a new employee, I accidentally shredded important documents.

準備口頭報告／簡報
prepare for one's presentation

預約會議室
book a room for a meeting

Time for a meeting.

請會議參與者出席會議
ask the conference participants to attend

PLAN

出席（晨間）會議
attend a (morning) meeting

準備好資料並分發給各位
prepare one's material and distribute copies

SENTENCES TO USE

這是Olivia第一次準備簡報，她非常緊張。
It was Olivia's first time to prepare for a presentation and she was very nervous.

我因為忘記預約會議室而被老闆罵了。
I was scolded by my boss for forgetting to reserve a meeting room.

那位最年輕的同事在會議前複印並分發文件。
The youngest co-worker makes copies and distributes the documents before the meeting.

進行小組會議
have a meeting with the team

在會議中發言
speak at a
meeting

持相反意見
have / show / take
an opposite opinion / view

與海外客戶進行視訊會議
hold a videoconference
with overseas clients / customers

集思廣益
collect / gather each
other's opinions

提出／討論未來的策略
come up with / discuss future strategies

結束會議
end the meeting

由於時差的關係，與海外客戶舉行視訊會議並不是一件容易的事。
Due to the time difference, it is not easy to hold a videoconference with overseas customers.

讓我們收集意見並提出未來的策略。
Let's gather our opinions and come up with a future strategy.

A 我們準備好要開始會議了。
▶ We are good to go with the meeting.

B 好的，今天的會議是關於克里斯先生昨天參與會議的成果報告。
● Okay, today's meeting is about an outcome report of the meeting Mr. Chris attended yesterday.

克里斯先生，請開始進行簡報。
● Please proceed with the presentation, Mr. Chris.

A 非常感謝。 昨天，我們向 XYZ 的策略規劃團隊介紹了我們的服務並做了一場簡報，反應非常好。
▶ Thank you very much. Yesterday, we introduced our service to XYZ's strategic planning team and demonstrated it, and the response was very good.

他們仔細查看過產品的規格，並詢問了許多有關技術的問題。
▶ They carefully checked the specifications of the product and asked a lot of questions about the technology as well.

之後我們一起共進午餐，他們一直在稱讚我們的產品。
▶ We had lunch together afterwards, and they kept complimenting us on our products.

B 噢，看來一切都很順利。
● Oh, it seems like everything is going well.

克里斯先生，您認為事情進展得如何？
● Mr. Chris, how do you think things will proceed?

A 首先，他們的團隊領導人要求在向他們的執行長報告之前，召開一場有關這項技術的工程師會議。
▶ First, their team leader requested an engineer meeting regarding the technology before reporting to their CEO.

看來他們的開發者會在召開技術轉移會議後才做報告。
▶ It seems like their developers will report after conducting a meeting on technology transfer.

B 了解。這項技術的相關細節包括我們的專利技術和很多機密資訊，所以我們需要他們先簽署 NDA（保密協議），然後再進行會議。

● I see. Details related to the technology include our patented technology and a lot of confidential information, so we need them to sign the NDA (Non-Disclosure Agreement) first and then proceed with the meeting.

A 是的，女士。我已經將保密協議相關的電子郵件發給他們的團隊領導人，並決定在開會前簽好。

▶ Yes, ma'am. I've already emailed their team leader about the confidentiality agreement and decided to sign it before the meeting.

如果工程師會議順利的話，下一步該如何進行呢？

▶ If the engineer meeting goes well, how should we proceed to the next step?

B 之後，向我們的代表做報告，並準備一份正式的備忘錄提案。

● After that, report to our representatives and prepare an official MOU proposal.

如果對方同意這份備忘錄，請雙方執行長再開個會、簽定備忘錄並分發新聞稿內容。

● If the other party agrees to the MOU, have another meeting for both CEOs to sign the MOU and distribute the contents for press release.

A 是的，女士。 我想，待備忘錄簽定之後會進行細部的協商。

▶ Yes, ma'am. I guess the detailed negotiations will proceed after the MOU is signed.

我會照你說的順序進行。

▶ I will proceed in the order you said.

C06U4.mp3

詢問客戶的意見
consult a client

進行顧客滿意度調查
conduct a customer
satisfaction survey

給客戶發個感謝的訊息
send a thank-you message
to the customer

與客戶會面
meet a client

與客戶交換名片
exchange business
cards with a client

解說給客戶聽
explain to the
client

回答客戶的問題
answer the client's
questions

與客戶喝咖啡
have / drink a coffee
with one's client

與客戶簽約
sign a contract with
the client

分析顧客消費模式
analyze customer
consumption patterns

SENTENCES TO USE

大公司都會進行一年一度的顧客滿意度調查並試著去了解顧客。
Major companies conduct an annual customer satisfaction survey and try to understand customers.

我們通常在會議前會交換名片，但我們都用完了。
We usually exchange business cards before meetings, but we ran out.

在簽訂合約之前，我的團隊必須向客戶解釋我們銷售額下降的原因。
My team had to explain to the client about our decrease in sales before signing a contract.

我和客戶在辦公室洽談之後去喝了一杯咖啡。
I had a coffee with my client after our consultation in the office.

務必在產品製造之前分析顧客消費模式。
Make sure to analyze customer consumption patterns before making the products.

C06U5.mp3

上班不進公司
work outside
of the office

去出差
go on a
business trip

四處拜訪客戶
go around doing
business

以電子郵件發送估價單
e-mail
an estimate

說明不同訂購量
的價格差異
explain the price
difference in order
quantities

將收據轉交會計部
pass one's receipt on to the
accounting department

申請已支付金額的報銷
get reimbursed for
one's expenses

包裝產品
package the
product

開發票
issue an invoice
/ a waybill

用快遞寄送…
deliver ~ by / send
~ through courier

比較競品的優缺點
compare pros and cons
with competitor's products

SENTENCES TO USE

Sally很高興能去香港出差一個星期。
Sally was excited to go on a one-week business trip to Hong Kong.

我本該在開會前 email 給客戶一份估價單，但我忘了。
I was supposed to email an estimate to the client before the meeting, but I forgot.

除非你把（帳單）收據交給會計部門，否則無法報銷。
Unless you pass the receipt on to the accounting department, you won't get reimbursed.

有一名員工包裝產品並以快遞寄送出去。
There is an employee who packages the product and sends it through courier.

他與競爭對手的產品進行了優缺點比較，並透過傳真發送這份報告。
He compared pros and cons in the competitor's products and sent the report by fax.

6 午休時間

12:30 PM

午休一下
take a lunch break

在自助餐廳用餐
eat in the cafeteria

想想和誰一起吃午餐
think about who to have lunch with

決定要吃什麼
decide what to eat

不吃午餐
skip lunch

吃午餐便當
eat a box(ed) lunch

SENTENCES TO USE

我擔心一想到要和老闆共進午餐我就胃不舒服。
I'm afraid the thought of having lunch with my boss gives me an upset stomach.

我總是在想午餐要吃什麼。
I always think about what to eat for lunch.

艾娃開始不吃午餐，並在午餐時間參加普拉提課程。
Ava started skipping lunch and taking Pilates lessons during lunch hours.

C06U6.mp3

到公司附近的一家餐廳用餐
<u>go to</u> / <u>visit</u> a restaurant near one's company

利用午休時間自我學習成長
self-develop during lunch hours

小睡一下
take a nap

在公司周圍走走
take a walk around the company

午餐後喝杯咖啡休息一下
take a coffee break after lunch

我們喜歡去公司附近道地的小餐館吃午餐。
We like to visit small local food restaurants near our company for lunch.

午餐後，有些員工要小睡片刻，而有些要喝杯咖啡休息一下。
Several employees either take a nap or take a coffee break after lunch.

人事考核

獲得獎勵金
<u>get</u> / <u>receive</u>
a bonus

招募新進員工
recruit new <u>employees</u>
/ <u>workers</u>

Good job...

跟公司報告優良績效
report achievements
to the company

辭去…（某職位）
resign (from)

You are promoted.

獲得升遷（以表彰某人工作上的出色表現）
<u>be</u> / <u>get</u> promoted (in recognition of one's achievements)

協商薪資待遇
negotiate for one's salary

（從某職位）退休
retire (from)

SENTENCES TO USE

Chloe獲得晉升以及獎金以表彰其工作上的成就。
Chloe was promoted in recognition of her achievements along with a bonus.

她在退休前一直都沒有機會協商她的薪資待遇。
She never got the chance to negotiate for her salary before she retired.

被解雇
<u>be</u> / <u>get</u> <u>fired</u> / <u>dismissed</u>

遞交辭呈
hand in one's resignation

換工作
change one's job;
move to a different company

接受公司法務團隊的審核
get audited by the
company's legal team

遭到停職處分
（作為一種紀律措施）
receive suspension
(as a disciplinary measure)

遭到減薪
get a <u>pay cut</u> /
disposition of salary
reduction

被送去公司的紀律委員會
be <u>sent</u> / <u>referred</u> / <u>submitted</u>
to the corporate disciplinary
committee

我被前公司不當解雇，且訴訟還沒結束。
I was wrongfully dismissed from my previous workplace and the trials are not over yet.

我寧願跳槽到另一家公司也不願接受降薪。
I'd rather move to a different company than get a pay cut.

A 你去年的表現非常好。恭喜你在兩年內提前獲得晉升。

▶ Your performance last year was very good. Congratulations on your early promotion in 2 years.

B 感謝您。我相信有這樣的結果是因為我能夠與優秀的團隊成員一起工作。

● I appreciate that. I believe the results came out as such because I was able to work with good team members.

A 太客氣了！從加班的時數以及銷售業績來看，我可以想見你們團隊多麼努力。

▶ How modest! I can see how hard your team worked through the overtime hours and sales performances.

去年績效獎金將依公司規定於下個季度末個別發放。

▶ Bonus for last year's performance will be paid separately at the end of next quarter in accordance with the company's regulations.

B 太感謝了。當我從前公司跳槽過來時，我還曾擔心自己能否做好這份工作，但現在我有一份適合我的工作，可以享受我的工作生活。

● Thank you so much. I was worried about whether I could do this job well when I moved from my previous company, but now I am enjoying my work life with a job that suits me.

A 是的，哈伯斯先生，我們也很高興與像您這樣的人一起工作。言歸正傳，您期待明年的薪資加多少？

▶ Yes, we are also happy to be working with someone like you, Mr. Harbers. To get to the point, how much increase do you expect in next year's salary?

B 既然我讓您看到了去年的業績成果，且在這次專案中拿到一張重要的合約，若您不介意的話，我想要求以我目前薪資為基礎加薪三成。

● Since I showed you the result of last year's performance and recently landed a big contract for a project this time, if you don't mind, I'd like to ask for a 30% increase from my current salary.

A 加薪 30%？這比我們想像還要高。不過，去年的表現確實很好，所以我們會積極審閱。您還有其他要求嗎？

▶ 30% increase? It's higher than what we were thinking. However, it is true that last year's performance was very good, so we will review it positively. Do you have any other requirements?

B 是的，我希望比去年增加 5 天的休假。另外，如果您可以將專案合約的獎金提高 20%，我將不勝感激。

● Yes, I'd like 5 more days of vacation added on to my previous year. Also, I would appreciate it if you could raise the bonus for the project contracts by 20% more.

A 是的，我認為休假日的部分我們是可以做到的，但獎金的增加對我們來說可能是負擔。我們建議另外增加 5 天休假、加薪 25%、獎金增加 10%。你認為呢？

▶ Yes, I think we can do that for the vacation days, but the bonus increase could be a burden for us. We would like to suggest an additional 5 days of vacation days, a 25% salary increase, and a 10% bonus increase. What do you think?

B 嗯…我可以考慮幾天再回覆你嗎？事實上，有人給我更優渥的條件來換工作，所以我的加薪提議是最低限度了。那既然協商並不如我想像那樣，我需要一點時間思考。

● Hmm… Can I think about it for a few days and get back to you? In fact, I was offered a job change under better conditions, so I suggested a minimum increase. Since the negotiation didn't go through as I thought it would, I need some time to think.

A 沒問題的。請考慮一下，然後下週三見面時再讓我們知道您的決定。感謝你的努力付出。

▶ No problem. Please think about it and let us meet next Wednesday to tell us your decision. Thank you for your efforts.

撰寫每日工作日誌
<u>keep</u> / <u>draw up</u> a daily work log

加班
work <u>after hours</u> / <u>overtime</u>

整理桌面
organize the top of one's desk

• clock in 用於上班時，
clock out 用於下班時

上班／下班打卡
clock <u>in</u> / <u>out</u>

下班後與朋友碰面
meet up with a friend after work

工作與生活達到平衡
have work-life balance

SENTENCES TO USE

我下班前幾乎不會忘記寫每天的工作日誌。
I rarely forget to draw up my daily work log before I get off work.

Jaime 對於每個月底都要加班這件事感到厭倦。
Jaime is tired of working overtime at the end of every month.

如果我們都能準時下班，我們也許可以實現工作與生活的完美平衡。
We probably will have perfect work-life balance if we leave work on the dot.

C06U8.mp3

下班後去健身
<u>go workout</u> / <u>exercise</u> after work

學習演奏樂器
learn to play an instrument

跟同事一起吃晚餐
get together for dinner with one's co-worker

跟同事喝一杯
have a drink with one's co-worker

去唱卡拉OK
go to karaoke

準時下班
leave work on the dot

下班後和同事去喝一杯還可以，但絕不能和我老闆一起。
It's okay to have a drink with my co-worker after work, but never with my boss.

我們這組通常會去打保齡球或去唱卡拉OK。
Our team usually goes bowling or goes to karaoke.

醫院

HOSPITAL

醫院事務

C07U1.mp3

順道去一趟當地診所／醫院
stop by a <u>local</u> <u>clinic</u> / <u>hospital</u>

* 在美國的醫院必須
出示這張保險卡

出示醫療保險卡
show one's medical insurance card

接受第一次的健康檢查
receive one's first medical examination

等候護士叫名
wait for a nurse to call

預約醫師看診
make <u>an appointment</u> <u>with the doctor</u> / <u>a doctor's appointment</u>

Doctor's Note

向一家綜合醫院
提交醫生的醫療證明
<u>submit</u> / <u>give</u> a doctor's note to a general hospital

拿到處方箋
<u>receive</u> / <u>get</u> a prescription

結清醫療費用
<u>settle</u> / <u>pay for</u> the medical expenses

收到醫療帳單收據
<u>receive</u> / <u>get</u> a receipt for medical expenses

開診斷證明
issue a <u>medical certificate</u> / <u>written diagnosis</u>

INSURANCE

向保險公司申請醫療費用給付
charge an insurance company for medical expenses; claim on the insurance

辦理住院手續
go through <u>procedures for hospitalization</u> / <u>the hospitalization process</u>

SENTENCES TO USE

請安靜地坐著，等待護士或醫生叫您。
Please sit still and wait until a nurse or a doctor calls on you.

您來之前必須先掛號，因為這裡並非隨來隨看的診所。
You need to make a doctor's appointment before you come because this is not a walk-in clinic.

這家當地診所的資源有限，因此您必須攜帶這份醫師證明去綜合醫院。
This local clinic has limited resources so you must take this doctor's note to a general hospital.

拿到醫療帳單收據後我們就去拿處方箋吧。
Let's go get the prescription after we get the receipt for our medical expenses.

我現在必須辦理住院手續。
I need to go through the hospitalization process right now.

2 就診

C07U2.mp3

進入就診室
go / walk into the
doctor's office

接受診治
receive / get medical
treatment / care

How are you feeling?

詢問病患的健康狀況
ask about health state of a patient;
inquire about a patient's health

用聽診器進行診療
examine / check
with a stethoscope

把脈；檢查脈搏
take / check for
a pulse

量體溫
take one's
temperature

接受核磁共振檢查
take
an MRI

* take an X-ray
是指「照 X 光」

看 X 光照片
take a look at
an X-ray

開一張醫師證明
write / make a doctor's note

說明病患診治的結果
explain the results of the
treatment to the patient

與其他專科醫師合作
cooperate with
other specialists

SENTENCES TO USE

如果您想接受醫療照護，請誠實告知您的健康狀況。
If you want to receive medical care, be honest about your health state.

護士，您能檢查一下這位車禍傷者的脈搏嗎？
Nurse, could you check for a pulse on the car accident victim?

在您進入醫師就診室之前，我們得先量一下您的體溫。
Let's take your temperature before you walk into the doctor's office.

我們必須看一下你的 X 光片，以確保你的手臂沒有骨折。
We need to take a look at your X-ray to make sure your arm is not broken.

您是否考量過醫生必須向病人解釋治療結果時的處境？
Have you considered the doctor's situation to explain the results of the treatment to the patient?

A 有什麼問題呢？
▶ What seems to be the problem?

B 我的左下胃已經好幾天有點輕微疼痛。
● I've had a slight pain in my lower left stomach for a few days.

我有噁心的感覺、會胸悶，小腹不時感覺刺痛。
● I feel nauseous and stuffy, and I feel stabbing pain in my lower abdomen from time to time.

A 您有慢性的消化系統疾病嗎？
▶ Do you have any chronic diseases in your digestive system?

B 嗯，我去年得過一次急性腸炎，但據我所知，我沒有慢性病。
● Well, I had acute enteritis once last year, but as far as I know, I don't have a chronic disease.

A 您最近有做過內視鏡檢查或超音波檢查嗎？
▶ Have you had an endoscopy or ultrasound recently?

B 兩個月前體檢的時候做了胃纖維鏡和大腸鏡檢查，但除了切除幾塊息肉外，沒有什麼大問題。
● I had a gastro fiberscope and a colonoscopy when I had a medical check-up two months ago, but there was no big problem other than having a few polyps removed.

A 好的。您最近是否飲酒過量、暴飲暴食或吃過生食？
▶ Okay. Have you been overdrinking, overeating, or have eaten raw food recently?

B 上週我去海邊玩，吃了海參和海螺生魚片。

● I went to the beach last week and ate sea cucumber and conch sashimi.

我想是在那之後讓我感到不舒服。

● I guess I feel uncomfortable after that.

A 你的排便狀況如何？

▶ How's your bowel movement?

B 我以前有嚴重的便秘，但這週我開始腹瀉。

● I used to have severe constipation, but I started having diarrhea this week.

A 我明白了。你很有可能是食物中毒，所以我給你開些藥，如果吃完之後還是感覺不舒服的話再回來做個徹底檢查。

▶ I see. It is most likely food poisoning, so I will prescribe you some medicine and you can come back for a thorough examination if you feel uncomfortable even after taking it.

B 好的，謝謝醫生。 這是在保險範圍內嗎？

● Okay, thank you doctor. Is this covered by insurance?

A 找外面的行政人員談談，他們會仔細地引導您。

▶ Have a talk with the administration staff outside and they will guide you in detail.

填寫健康調查表
fill out / write in a health survey

進行全身健康檢查／做體檢
get a full body / medical check-up

量體重
take / measure one's weight

量身高
take / measure one's height

量血壓
take / measure one's blood pressure

檢查心律
check one's heart rate

SENTENCES TO USE

在與醫生見面之前，您必須填寫這份健康調查表。
You have to fill out this health survey before meeting the doctor.

在我體檢時，護士幫我量身高和體重。
The nurse measured my height and weight when I was getting a medical check-up.

要是您感到頭暈，我們人可來量一下您的血壓吧！
If you feel dizzy, why don't we take your blood pressure?

進行血液檢查
<u>take</u> / <u>do</u> a blood test

進行糞便／尿液的檢查；進行糞便檢驗
have one's <u>bowels</u> / <u>urine</u> tested;
<u>make</u> / <u>have</u> a stool test

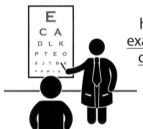

檢查視力
have one's eyes
<u>examined</u> / <u>tested</u> /
<u>checked</u>; get an
eye exam

進行聽力測試
have one's hearing <u>examined</u> / <u>tested</u>
/ <u>checked</u>; get an audiometry

進行…超音波檢查
<u>get</u> / <u>have</u> an
ultrasound (on ~)

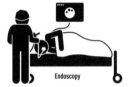

進行內視鏡檢查
<u>have</u> / <u>undergo</u> an endoscopy
/ <u>endoscope</u> procedure

他必須進行血液檢查，以確定自己是否受到感染。
He needs to take a blood test and find out whether he is infected.

我要去醫院做甲狀腺超音波檢查。
I am going to the hospital to get an ultrasound on my thyroid.

在手臂上打針／注射
give <u>an injection</u> / <u>a shot</u>
in one's arm

在手臂內加裝靜脈導管
get an IV (intravenous) in one's arm;
be put on an IV (intravenous)

進行急救措施
give first aid; take emergency
measures; seek emergency care

開處方
prescribe

整理患者病歷
organize a patient chart

SENTENCES TO USE

我學會如何給患者進行急救措施。
I learned how to give first aid to those in need.

這種藥通常是為了治療胃潰瘍而開的。
The drug is usually prescribed for a gastric ulcer.

C07U4.mp3

為某人做例行檢查
<u>do</u> / <u>make</u> one's rounds

指示病患做身體鍛鍊
prescribe exercise; <u>present</u> / <u>give</u>
prescription of exercise

接受⋯的手術
<u>go through</u> / <u>undergo</u> a ~ surgery

進行⋯的手術
perform a ~ surgery; operate on ~

被宣告死亡
be pronounced dead

宣告某人死亡
pronounce one's death

進行驗屍
<u>do</u> / <u>perform</u> an autopsy

病人的背部手術恢原後，醫生指示要做身體鍛鍊。
The doctor prescribed exercise after the patient recovered from his back surgery.

Noah小時候曾做過心臟手術。
Noah went through a heart surgery when he was a child.

不幸的是，在他能夠被送往醫院之前就被宣告死亡了。
Unfortunately, he was pronounced dead before he could get to the hospital.

我們需要進行驗屍，找出病人猝死的原因。
We need to do an autopsy to find out the reason why the patient suddenly became deceased.

…（身體部位）疼痛

have a(n) ~ ache; feel / have a pain in one's ~

劇烈頭痛

have a throbbing headache

偏頭痛

have a migraine

身體酸痛

have a body ache

感冒

catch a cold

感到…（身體部位）陣陣刺痛

have / feel a throbbing ache / pain in one's ~

感到…（身體部位）麻痺

have / feel a numbness in one's ~; feel ~ is asleep

感覺…（身體部位）不舒服

feel uncomfortable in one's ~

…（身體部位）燙傷

get a burn on ~; burn one's ~

…（身體部位）抽筋

have a spasm / cramp in ~

罹患了…（疾病）

come down with the ~

SENTENCES TO USE

我在運動課程之後感覺肌肉劇烈疼痛。
I have an intense muscle ache after my workout session.

請不要在屋裡亂跑，我頭很痛耶。
Please don't run around in the house, I have a throbbing headache.

坐了幾個小時後，他的腿麻痺了。
He had a numbness in his legs after sitting down for hours.

我小時候曾經被溢出的滾燙熱水燙傷了手指。
I burned my fingers by spilling boiling water when I was little.

Amelia 被雨淋濕後得了流感。
Amelia came down with the flu after she got wet in the rain.

C07U5.mp3

冒冷汗，夜間盜汗
break out in a cold
sweat; have night sweats

咳嗽，發出咳嗽聲
cough;
have a cough

喉嚨有痰；喉嚨沙啞
have phlegm;
have a frog in
one's throat

胃不舒服；消化不良
have an upset stomach
/ a stomachache;
suffer from indigestion

感到噁心，覺得想吐
feel / get nausea / sick /
queasy; feel nauseous

感到暈眩
feel dizzy
/ light-headed

發燒
run / have a fever

罹患黃疸症
have jaundice

感到搔癢，會癢
have / get an itch

呼吸困難
have difficulty
breathing

流鼻血
have / get a bloody
nose / nosebleed

對…有過敏反應
have an allergic
reaction to ~

SENTENCES TO USE

這整個週末我都一直盜汗，且身體酸痛。
I had night sweats and body aches throughout the weekend.

他整個星期一直在咳嗽。
He has had a cough all week.

我昏過去之前有一點噁心的感覺。
I was feeling a little queasy before I passed out.

你看到他的臉了嗎？他一定有黃疸症！
Did you see his face? He definitely has jaundice!

我兒子一有過敏反應就會發癢。
My son gets an itch whenever he has an allergic reaction.

將…（傷口等的邊緣）
縫合／癒合
<u>stitch up</u> ~ / <u>suture</u> ~

切除腫瘤
<u>excise</u> / <u>remove</u>
a tumor

接受剖腹手術
<u>get</u> / <u>undergo</u>
a laparotomy

接受輸血
<u>get</u> / <u>receive</u> a blood
transfusion

進行切片檢查
<u>take</u> / <u>do</u>
a biopsy

• 將…裂開的部分
重新癒合
將…連結
<u>join</u> / <u>connect</u> ~

進行…的移植
<u>transplant</u> ~;
have a ~ transplant

進行物理療法
<u>carry out</u> / <u>get</u> / <u>do</u>
physical therapy

服用藥物；以藥物治療
take medication;
be treated with
<u>medication</u> / <u>drugs</u>

檢視康復／手術過程
check the <u>progress of</u>
<u>rehabilitation</u> / <u>operation</u>
/ <u>surgery</u>

術後復原過程順利
progress after surgery
is good; postoperative
recovery has been good

SENTENCES TO USE

我媽媽在廚房割傷了手指之後，必須將手指的傷口縫合。
My mom had to get her finger stitched up after she cut her finger in the kitchen.

我們必須進行肝臟切片手術，以確認它是良性還是惡性的。
We need to do a liver biopsy to determine if it's benign or malignant.

他在意外發生之後就必須持續接受物理治療。
He had to continue with physical therapy after the accident.

我們下週來檢視一下您的復原進度。
Let's check your progress of rehabilitation next week.

Eugene 很高興聽到他術後復原順利。
Eugene was grateful to hear that his postoperative recovery has been great.

接受癌症治療
receive treatments / get treated for cancer

接受化療
get / undergo / receive chemotherapy

上了石膏
wear a cast

針灸治療
get acupuncture; get / be ~ treated with acupucture

在…繫上繃帶
put a bandage on ~; bandage one's ~

將傷口消毒
disinfect one's wound

將…（某人）全身麻醉
put ~ under general anesthesia

使…（某人）局部麻醉
put ~ under local / regional anesthesia

接受心理諮商（治療）
receive counseling therapy / treatment

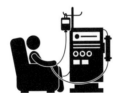

進行洗腎
be put on (kidney) dialysis

將…（身體部位）截斷
amputate one's ~

坐上輪椅
be in a wheelchair

SENTENCES TO USE

我祖母過去曾去針灸治療她的手腕。
My grandmother used to get her wrist treated with acupuncture.

在包紮傷口之前我們先消毒一下。
Let's disinfect that wound before we bandage it.

她不需要全身麻醉，簡單的局部麻醉就夠了。
There is no need to put her under general anesthesia, simple local anesthesia will suffice.

你女兒最好去接受諮商治療，因為她看起來壓力很大。
Your daughter'd better go to counseling therapy since she seems to be under a lot of stress.

軍醫無奈，只能在戰場上截掉這名士兵的腿。
The medic had no choice but to amputate the soldier's leg on the battle field.

C07U7.mp3

打 119
call 119
* 美國的緊急電話是 911。

進行（口對口）人工呼吸
give mouth-to-mouth / a kiss of life

進行心肺復甦術（CPR）
do / perform / give CPR (cardiopulmonary resuscitation)

戴上氧氣罩
put on an oxygen respirator / a ventilator

使用人工呼吸器
use a ~ inhaler / puffer

進行止血
Bleeding
stop the bleeding

在…（身體部位）進行按摩／推拿
massage / rub down one's ~

失去意識
lose one's consciousness; go black; pass / black out; faint

恢復意識
regain / recover one's consciousness

使用 AED（自動體外顫器）裝置
use an AED (automated external defibrillator) device

用救護車送去急診室
go to the ER (emergency room) by ambulance / in an ambulance

SENTENCES TO USE

學習給孩子做心肺復甦術是非常重要的。
It is important to learn how to perform CPR on a child.

Jenny 總是隨身攜帶人工呼吸器，以防氣喘發作。
Jenny always carries an inhaler in case of an asthma attack.

我必須先進行止血才能縫合。
I need to stop the bleeding before I can stitch it up.

James 在前往急診室的救護車上就昏倒了。
James passed out in the ambulance on the way to the ER.

按摩全身可以幫助他們恢復意識。
Massaging one's whole body helps them regain consciousness.

8 藥局

C07U8.mp3

將處方交給藥劑師
hand in / give
a prescription to
a pharmacist

詢問某種藥物的效用
inquire / ask about
the effectiveness
/ effect of a medicine

檢查藥物治療週期
check the
medication cycle

購買家用藥物
buy a household
medicine

付醫藥費
pay for a medicine
/ meds

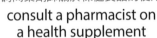

詢問藥劑師關於保健食品的使用
consult a pharmacist on
a health supplement

要求使用／準備藥粉
ask for powdered medicine /
ask to prepare powdered medicine

得到用藥方式的說明
get an explanation
of how to take the
medicine

請藥劑師說明藥物的副作用；聆聽藥劑師
說明藥物的副作用
have a pharmacist explain the
side effects; listen to a pharmacist
explaining the side effects

前往24小時營業的藥局
visit / go to a pharmacy
open 24 hours a day

SENTENCES TO USE

你給藥劑師處方時為什麼不問一下有什麼副作用？
Why don't you ask about the side effects when you give the prescription to the pharmacists?

我需要買一些家用藥品以供緊急用途。
I need to buy several household medicines in case of emergency.

嬰兒和幼兒服用粉狀藥物，因為他們很難吞嚥藥片。
Babies and toddlers take powdered medicine because it's hard for them to swallow pills.

由於您目前的病情，服用保健品需先諮詢藥劑師。
You need to consult a pharmacist first on taking health supplements due to your current medication.

我找到了一家24小時甚至週末也有營業的藥局！
I found a pharmacy that opens 24 hours and even on the weekends!

CHAPTER

8

銀行

BANK

銀行

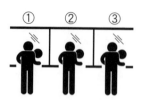

查看櫃檯前的等候人數
check the <u>number of people</u>
<u>waiting</u> / <u>waiting list</u> at the counter

拿到號碼牌後等待叫號
wait for one's turn after <u>taking a number</u>
/ <u>getting a number ticket</u>

透過…驗證身分
verify oneself <u>through</u> / <u>with</u> ~;
confirm one's identification through ~

BANK ATM

從提款機領現
withdraw cash
from an ATM

關閉銀行帳戶
close a bank account

開一個存款帳戶／定期儲蓄帳戶
<u>set up</u> / <u>open</u> a deposit account / <u>an installment savings account</u>

SENTENCES TO USE

你有看到提款機了嗎？ 我必須領些現金。
Do you see an ATM? I have to withdraw some cash.

為了關閉她的銀行帳戶，Mila 透過一張有照片的身份證件來驗證自己的身份。
In order to close her bank account, Mila verified herself through a photo ID.

存錢／提款／轉帳
<u>save</u> / <u>withdraw</u> / <u>transfer</u> money

認購定期定額基金
subscribe to an installment fund

將紙鈔換成零錢
<u>change</u> / <u>break</u> a bill into coins

存摺換新
update one's bankbook

換匯
exchange money

繳稅／繳帳單
pay <u>taxes</u> / <u>bills</u>

有保險箱
<u>have</u> / <u>get</u> a <u>safe-deposit</u>
/ <u>safety-deposit</u> box

Michael 在認購定期定額基金之前會諮詢銀行經理。
Michael will consult a bank manager before he subscribes to an installment fund.

我的父母已經很多年沒有將銀行存摺換新了。
My parents have not updated their bankbooks for years.

糟糕，我忘了要先去銀行換鈔！
Oh no, I forgot to exchange money at the bank beforehand!

網路銀行

登入網銀
log <u>in</u> / <u>on</u> to the bank website

啟用行動銀行 app
open the mobile <u>banking</u> / <u>bank</u> app

發給／更新／更換認證憑證
<u>issue</u> / <u>renew</u> / <u>change</u> an authentication certificate
從另一家機構註冊認證憑證
register an authentication certificate from another agency
匯出／複製行動憑證
<u>export</u> / <u>copy</u> mobile certificates

輸入指紋／密碼／圖樣來登入
<u>enter</u> / <u>use</u> a <u>fingerprint</u> /
<u>password</u> / <u>pattern</u> to log in

SENTENCES TO USE

Dan 已經有一段時間沒有打開他的行動銀行 app 了，所以他必須先進行升級才能使用。
Dan has not opened his mobile banking app for a while, so he has to upgrade it before using it.

我必須每年更新一次認證憑證。
I have to renew an authentication certificate once a year.

選擇你要進行交易的帳戶
<u>select</u> / <u>choose</u> the account you
want to transact with

選擇存款／提款／轉帳交易
<u>select</u> / <u>choose</u> a <u>deposit</u> / <u>withdrawal</u>
/ <u>transfer</u> / <u>remit</u> transaction

輸入金額
enter one's amount

輸入密碼／OTP 碼（一次性動態密碼）
enter <u>a password</u> /
<u>an OTP (one-time programmable) number</u>

查看帳戶餘額
check one's balance

開一個線上／行動帳戶
<u>create</u> / <u>make</u> <u>an online</u> / <u>a mobile</u> account

糟糕！我選了存款交易而不是提款！
Oops! I chose a deposit transaction instead of withdrawal!

我多次輸入錯誤的密碼，現在我的帳戶被鎖起來了。
I entered a wrong password several times and now my account is locked.

我查了一下餘額，我的月薪還沒存入。
I checked my balance and my monthly salary has not been deposited.

她為了證券交易開了一個線上帳戶。
She made an online account for stock trading purposes.

審查貸款資格
**undergo a loan prequalification;
get prequalified for a loan**

查看／審查個人信用資料
check / undergo one's
personal credit information

申請貸款
apply for a loan

查看利率
check / review the interest rate

填寫貸款同意書
draw up / fill in a loan agreement

設定擔保品
**set up a security /
collateral for a loan**

提供共同擔保（人）；
承擔某人的債務風險
**give joint surety;
underwrite one's debt / loan**

簽本票（或 IOU）
**draw / write up
a promissory note / an IOU**

SENTENCES TO USE

無論我們查看多少次您的個人信用資料，您都不符貸款資格。
No matter how many times we check your personal credit information, you are not qualified for a loan.

我要在填寫貸款同意書之前查看一下利率。
I am going to check the interest rate before filling in a loan agreement.

承擔他人的債務風險是不明智的，即使是為了家人。
It is unwise to underwrite one's debts even if it's for a family.

設定還款時間表
schedule <u>repayment</u>
/ <u>pay-back</u> of a loan

償還貸款的本金／利息
<u>repay</u> / <u>pay back</u> the <u>principal</u> /
<u>interest</u> of one's loan

要求調降利率
demand an interest rate cut;
demand for a cut in interest rates

申請破產
file for
bankruptcy

負債累累，背負沉重債務
drown in debt; be up to one's
ears in debt; be in a huge debt

獲得房屋貸款
take out a mortgage (loan)

獲得浮動利率／固定利率的房貸
take out a <u>variable</u> / <u>floating-rate</u>
/ <u>fixed-rate</u> mortgage (loan)

我每個月要支付我們房貸的本金及利息是多少？
How much do I pay in principal and interest every month for our mortgage payment?

你不應該待在那間公司，因為那公司債務累累。
You should not work there since that company is drowning in debt.

A　你好。我要轉帳。
▶ Hello. I'd like to transfer some money.

B　午安，先生。首先，請出示身分證中以確認您的身分。
● Good afternoon, sir. First, I would like to confirm your identification with an ID.

A　好的，在這兒。
▶ Yes, here it is.

B　謝謝，確認完成。
● Thank you. It's been confirmed.

我要幫您將 2000 美元轉到寫在這的帳戶嗎？
● Should I help you transfer two thousand dollars to the account written here?

A　是的，麻煩了。我的帳戶有多少餘額？
▶ Yes, please. How much balance do I have in my account?

B　轉帳後您的餘額將是 4,500 美元。
● Your balance will be at 4,500 dollars after the transfer.

A　謝謝。然後我想要諮詢貸款事宜。
▶ Thank you. And I'd like to get a loan consultation please.

B　好的，先生。您要貸款多少？
● Yes, sir. How much loan are you in need?

A　我想申請 30,000 美元的個人信貸。利率是多少？
▶ I'd like to take 30,000 dollars on a personal credit loan. What is the interest rate?

B　沒問題。 我們會在核實您的個人信用資料後告知您利率的細節。
● No problem. We can inform you of the details of the interest rate after checking your personal credit information.

您可以填寫一下這份同意書嗎？
● Could you fill out the consent form?

A　我在這邊簽名嗎？
▶ Do I sign here with my name on it?

B 沒錯。根據結果顯示,您是我們銀行信用等級低的貴賓,因此貸款限額為 20,000 美元,利率為 7.2%。

● That is correct. According to the result, you are our bank VIP with a low credit rating, so the loan limit is 20,000 dollars and the interest rate will be 7.2%.

A 7.2%?比我預期還高。有什麼辦法可以降低利率嗎?

▶ 7.2%? That's higher than I expected. Is there any way to lower the interest rate?

B 若您用我們的個人帳戶設立薪轉帳戶,您將可調降 0.3%,每個月附卡的使用超過 300 美元的話將可再降 0.2%。

● If you set up a payroll transfer account with our personal account, you will receive 0.3%, using more than 300 dollars per month for affiliated credit card usage will get you 0.2%.

由於您擁有我們銀行的認購帳戶,您將另外再獲得 0.2%,所以最終利率會是 6.5%。

● Since you have our bank's subscription account, you will receive an additional 0.2%, which will make the final interest rate 6.5%.

A 那麼,請繼續進行這 20,000 美元的貸款,以及 24 個月後清償的 6.5% 利率。

▶ Then, please proceed with a 20,000-dollar loan and full repayment after 24 months at an interest rate of 6.5%.

是不是要收取一筆提前清償的費用呢?

▶ Is there an early redemption charge?

B 沒有提前清償的費用。在約滿之前您都可以在任何時候還款。

● There is no early redemption charge, you can repay as much as you want before the end of the contract.

這是交易協議。貸款將在一小時內存入您的帳戶。謝謝您。

● Here's the transaction agreement. The loan will be deposited into your account within an hour. Thank you.

區公所 & 行政福利中心

投入／提出民眾陳情書
put in / file
a civil complaint

取得一份核發的戶口名簿
get a copy of one's resident
registration issued

申請護照
apply for
a passport

申請殘障人士證；取得殘障人士證
apply for the disability registration;
get registered as disable

取得核發的居留證
get one's resident
registration card reissued

提交遷入通知書給公務機關
notify the public office of the new address
(that one has moved to); give the public
office a moving-in notification

SENTENCES TO USE

我父親對於公共停車位的缺乏感到憤怒，因此提出一份民眾陳情書。
My father was furious about the lack of public parking spaces, so he put in a civil complaint.

在我們出國旅行之前我必須申請新的護照。
I need to apply for a new passport before our travel overseas.

你能幫那名男子申請殘障人士登記證以及殘障人士停車證嗎？
Could you help that man with his application for the disability registration and a disabled parking badge?

結婚／出生／死亡登記
register / report one's marriage / birth / death

申請政府補助
apply for a
government subsidy

參加公聽會（聽取政府政策簡報）
listen to a government policy
briefing / briefing session

申請營業登記證
apply for a
business license

取得核發的親屬關係證明書
get a family relation certificate
/ a certificate of family relation issued

我們好像前幾天才登記結婚，現在就來為兒子做出生登記了。
It seems like we registered our marriage only a few days ago, but now we came to report our son's birth.

Owen 在開餐廳之前，必須先到地方政府單位申請營業登記證。
Owen had to apply for a business license at the ward office before he could open his restaurant.

買郵票
<u>buy</u> / <u>purchase</u> a stamp

寄信／郵件／包裹
send a <u>letter</u> / <u>mail</u> / <u>parcel</u> / <u>package</u>

寄掛號
send by
registered mail

把信放入郵筒
put a letter in
the mailbox

用快遞寄送…
send ~ <u>through</u> / <u>by express</u>
/ <u>special delivery</u>

寄海外包裹
send an overseas parcel

以空運寄…
send ~ by <u>air mail</u>
/ <u>air</u> / <u>plane</u>

SENTENCES TO USE

我在國外留學的時候，曾經寄國際包裹到韓國。
When I was studying abroad, I used to send international parcels to Korea.

您得在掛號郵件送達時簽收。
You need to sign the registered mail upon its delivery.

與航空郵件相比，透過海運寄送包裹需要更長的時間。
It takes longer to ship a parcel by sea mail compared to sending by airmail.

C08U5.mp3

以海運寄送…
ship / send ~ by sea mail;
send ~ by ship / sea

使用郵政信箱
use a P. O. Box
(post office box)

購買郵政保險
take out post office
insurance; take up a post
office insurance policy

郵差將…送到
a postman delivers ~

用快捷（EMS）寄送…
send ~ by EMS
(Express Mail Service)

購買標準信封／寄件箱
buy / purchase a standard
envelope / box

要求隔日／當日到貨
request next-day / same-day delivery

Jason 的住所不太固定，所以使用郵政信箱。
Jason used a P. O. Box due to his irregular place of address.

我媽媽為我買了郵政保險。
My mother took out post office insurance for me.

A 來賓 331 號，請到 2 號窗口。
▶ Waiting number 331, please come to window #2.

B 您好，我這兩件要寄掛號。
● Hello, I'd like to send these two by registered mail.

A 沒問題。 請將您要寄送的郵件放在磅秤上。
▶ No problem. Please put each mail you want to send on the scale.

普掛郵件共 4 美元，需要 2-3 天送達。
▶ It's 4 dollars in total by general registered mail which takes 2-3 days to deliver.

如果要使用快捷郵件，價格為 6 美元，保證明天送達。
▶ And if you use express mail, it's 6 dollars with guaranteed delivery tomorrow.

B 那麼我就用快捷寄送。
● Then I will proceed with the express delivery.

A 好的。請明確寫下收件人地址及聯絡資訊。
▶ Okay. Please write down the recipient's address and contact information clearly.

B 我想把這箱寄到紐約，麻煩了。
● And I'd like to send this box to New York, please.

A 箱子裡是否有易燃物品、易碎物品或可能變質的食物呢？
▶ Is there any flammable substance, fragile item, or food that can go bad in the box?

B 沒有，都只是書本。
● No. These are just books.

A 箱子重量超過30公斤，無法寄送。
▶ The box weighs more than 30kg, so it cannot be delivered.

我知道造成不便，但你得重新包裝成兩箱來寄送。
▶ I know it's inconvenient, but you need to repackage it into two boxes to deliver it.

（10 分鐘後 Ten minutes later）

B 我重新包裝成兩箱了。
● I repackaged it in two.

A 一般運送約需要 3 天左右送達，一箱 5美元，快捷的話是一箱 9 美元，隔日送達。你要哪一種方式？
▶ The regular delivery takes about 3 days and is 5 dollars per box, and the express delivery is 9 dollars per box and will be delivered the next day. Which one would you like?

B 我用一般運送的服務。
● I'll use the regular delivery service.

A 總共是 22 美元。
▶ The total amount is 22 dollars.

請將卡片插入您面前的讀卡機。
▶ Please insert the card to the reader in front of you.

您需要收據嗎？
▶ Do you need a receipt?

B 是的，麻煩了。謝謝。
● Yes, please. Thank you.

CHAPTER

9

購物

SHOPPING

購物中心、超市與市場

列出購物清單／將…列入購物清單中
make one's shopping list /
put ~ on one's shopping list

取出購物推車／購物籃
take / pull out a shopping
cart / basket

挑選物品
choose goods

詢問…的價格
ask the price of ~

比較價格
compare prices

在展位免費試吃／喝／用
taste / sample / try a product
at the free-sample stand / booth;
try a free-sample at the booth

SENTENCES TO USE

哦，我忘了把牛奶和雞蛋列入購物清單了。
Oh, I forgot to put milk and eggs on the shopping list.

我媽媽在市場上挑選物品前會先比較價格。
My mother compares prices before choosing goods at the market.

Violet 在展位嘗試免費樣品，並將產品放入她的購物車中。
Violet tried a free-sample at the booth and put the products in her cart.

C09U1_1.mp3

將…放進購物推車／購物籃
put ~ in a <u>cart</u> / <u>basket</u>

討價還價
<u>bargain</u> / <u>haggle</u> with someone over the price

把…丟進去
throw in ~ / throw ~ in

使用自助結帳櫃台
use <u>a self-checkout counter</u> / <u>self-checkout</u>

把東西放在收銀台上
put things on the <u>counter</u>
/ <u>checkstand</u> / <u>register</u>

如果我買這番茄醬，可以免費給我一包義大利麵嗎？
Can you throw in a pack of pasta for free if I buy this tomato sauce?

如果您不想排隊，可以使用自助結帳櫃檯。
If you don't want to stand in line, you can use the self-checkout counter.

使用移動人行道
use a moving <u>walkway</u> / <u>sidewalk</u>

買食物垃圾袋
buy a food waste bag

將…放入購物袋中
put ~ in one's shopping bag

賺取回饋點數
<u>earn</u> / <u>collect</u>
reward points

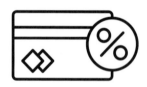

以會員權益卡獲得折扣
get a discount with a partner membership card

SENTENCES TO USE

Dana 使用移動人行道將她的購物車歸位。
Dana used a moving walkway to put her cart back in place.

我需要你幫我將我的雜貨放入購物袋並帶回家。
I need your help putting my groceries in my shopping bag and bringing it back home.

將…放在磅秤上秤重
weigh ~ on a scale

將購物車歸位
<u>put</u> / <u>return</u> the cart back in place

在顧客服務中心進行申訴
complain to the customer center;
bring up an issue with the customer center

到顧客服務中心領取贈送的物品
go to the customer center and
get a <u>giveaway</u> / <u>free gift</u>

將購買的物品放進後車箱中
put the purchased <u>goods</u> / <u>items</u> in the trunk;
load the trunk with purchased <u>goods</u> / <u>items</u>

安排購買物品的運送
have the purchased
<u>goods</u> / <u>items</u> delivered

將萵苣放入塑膠袋中，然後在磅秤上秤重。
Put the lettuce in a plastic bag before you weigh it on a scale.

不要忘記去顧客服務中心領取贈送的清潔劑。
Don't forget to go to the customer center and get a detergent as a free gift.

你能派些工作人員幫助那位老太太把她的雜貨放進後車箱嗎？
Could you get a staff to help that elderly lady to put her grocery in the trunk?

結帳與付款

掃描條碼
scan the bar code

以信用卡設定每月分期付款
make a monthly credit card installment <u>transaction</u> / <u>plan</u>

一次付清
pay in a lump sum; pay in full

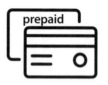

以儲值卡進行支付
<u>pay with</u> / <u>use</u> one's prepaid card

以現金支付
pay in cash

數零錢
count out one's change

要求現金收據
ask for a cash receipt

SENTENCES TO USE

我想以四個月分期零利率的方式付款。
I'd like to pay in an interest-free 4 month installment plan.

Ethan 用信用卡付款時，不自覺地要求提供現金收據。
Ethan unknowingly asked for a cash receipt when he paid with a credit card.

C09U2.mp3

用禮券（或禮品卡）支付
pay with a gift certificate (card)

將卡片遞給收銀員
<u>give</u> / <u>hand</u> one's card to the cashier

在讀卡機上簽名
sign a card reader

連同收據將卡歸還（給消費者）
<u>return</u> / <u>give back</u> the card with the receipt

用手機開啟電子支付卡
turn on an electronic card
with one's mobile phone

掃描手機付款
scan one's phone to <u>pay</u>
/ <u>make a payment</u>

將卡插入讀卡機中
insert the card into
the reader

我可以取消現金付款改用禮券支付嗎？
Can I cancel my cash payment and pay with a gift certificate instead?

哦，您有 Smile Pay 嗎？請在此掃描您的手機來付款。
Oh, you have Smile Pay? Please scan your phone here to make a payment.

您不必把卡片給我。您可以將卡片插入您面前的讀卡機。
You don't need to hand me the card, you can insert the card into the reader right in front of you.

A 即日起，我們提供新鮮美味的醃
製國產牛肋骨，每包 10 美元，僅
限 10 人購買！
▶ Starting now, we are offering
fresh and delicious marinated
domestic beef ribs for 10 dollars
per pack for only 10 people!

我們每人最多只允許攜帶 3 包，
所以要快點。
▶ We only allow a maximum of 3
packs per person, so hurry up.

B 我要兩包醃排骨！
● I'll take 2 packs of marinated
ribs!

今天有什麼好吃的豬肉？
● What pork is good today?

A 這個。來自伯克希爾的黑色五花
肉，昨天剛到，非常新鮮。
▶ Here you go. The black pork
belly from Berkshire just came in
yesterday, so it's very fresh.

它提供八折優惠價，到今天為止。
所以，您最好趁便宜的時候買。
▶ It's on a special 20% discount
until today. So, you'd better take
it when it's cheap.

B 那麼我也要兩包黑色五花肉。
● Then I will take 2 packs of
black pork belly, too.

現在什麼魚是當季的？
● Which fish is in season?

A 鯖魚正是時令，所以肥美可口。
▶ Mackerel is in season, so it's
fattened up and delicious.

平常是一尾 10 美元，但我們現在
有買 1 送 1 的活動。
▶ It's usually 10 dollars for one,
but we are currently having a
1+1 event.

B 那這我也要。
● I'll take it as well.

麻辣海鮮燉菜套餐好像有很多
種。您可以推薦一樣嗎？
● There seem to be many kinds
of spicy seafood stew meal kits.
Can you recommend one?

A 如果您喜歡吃辣，我推薦這種有
很多魷魚和貽貝的。
▶ If you like spicy food,
I recommend this one with a lot
of squid and mussels.

如果你您喜歡鹹味的，還有一種
有很多青蟹和小章魚的食品。
▶ If you like savory flavor, there is
also a product with a lot of blue
crabs and small octopus.

價格是雙倍，但由於是套餐所以
很受歡迎。
▶ The price is double, but
it's popular because of the
composition of the kit.

B 藍蟹套餐的價格超出我的預算，
我下次再買。
● The kit with the blue crab is
out of my price range, so I'll get it
next time.

我要支付我的雜貨費用，並且我
想用這張 3 美元的折價券並透過
文字傳送的方式來進行 50 美元以
上的消費。
● I'd like to pay for my groceries,
and I want to use this 3-dollar
discount coupon for purchases
over 50 dollars through text.

A 是的，使用優惠券後是 65 美元。
你需要塑膠袋嗎？要多收 10 美
分。
▶ Yes, it's 65 dollars with the
coupon applied. Do you need a
plastic bag? It's 10 cents extra.

B 沒關係。我帶了自己的購物袋。
什麼卡是免息的？
● That's okay. I brought my own
shopping bag. What card is
interest-free?

A 使用 YXZ 信用卡的話，您可以享
有長達 6 個月的免息優惠。
▶ You can get up to 6-month
interest-free with a YXZ credit
card.

B 我想以分 3 期零利率的方式付
款。我不需要收據。
● I'd like to pay in a 3-month
interest-free installment plan.
You can throw the receipt away.

A 好的，您希望如何使用您的積點？
▶ Yes, how would you like your
frequency points?

B 請將點數置入我本人 Kimberly
Hays 的電話號碼中，末四碼是
0355。我的貨可以用寄送的嗎？
● Please put the points under
the last four digits of my phone
number which is 0355 Kimberly
Hays. Can I get my groceries
delivered?

A 可以。麻煩在這裡寫下您的地
址，您的雜貨將在 30 分鐘內送達
您的住家。
▶ Yes. If you write down your
address here, you will receive
your groceries at home within 30
minutes.

B 好的，感謝您。
● Okay, thank you.

去百貨公司／購物商城／專賣店
go to a department
store / a shopping mall
/ an outlet

四處比價尋找…
shop around for ~

逛街／逛商店
go
window-shopping

瘋狂大採購
go on a shopping
/ spending spree

進去一家…店
go into a ~ store

查看…（商品）的狀況
check the condition
/ state of ~

詢問尺寸
ask about the size

（在試衣間）試穿…
try on ~; try ~ on
(in the fitting/dressing room)

查看價格
check the
price

查看…的庫存
check for ~'s
inventory;
check / find out
if ~ is in stock

已售罄
be
sold out

有新品的庫存
be stocked with new
products; be new in
stock

照鏡子（看是否合身）
check oneself
in the mirror

SENTENCES TO USE

Clara（本來）要去百貨公司買個錢包，但最後只是逛了逛。
Clara went to a department store to buy a purse but ended up window-shopping.

我們去專賣店看看有什麼新品吧。
Let's go to the outlet to check out what's new in stock.

我的家人每個季節都會瘋狂購物。
My family goes on a shopping spree every season.

我走進一家鞋店，問店員是否有限量鞋庫存。
I walked into a shoe store and asked the clerk if they had a limited edition shoe in stock.

我可以試穿這件襯衫和褲子嗎？
Can I please try this shirt and pants on?

找尋物美價廉的商品
**look for bargains;
look for merchandise on sale**

量合身的尺寸
**take (one's)
measurements**

尋找…（某商品）的不同顏色／尺寸
**look for ~ in
a different <u>color</u> / <u>size</u>**

排隊等候
<u>wait</u> / <u>stand</u> in line

詢問付現是否有折扣
**ask if there is a
cash discount**

購買比較不貴的某物
**buy something less
<u>expensive</u> / <u>pricey</u>**

詢問／確認是否可以寄送
（或運送）
**<u>ask</u> / <u>check</u> if delivery
is possible**

取得停車優惠券
**get one's parking
validated; get a parking
<u>voucher</u> / <u>discount</u>**

聽取退款政策說明
**<u>get</u> / <u>listen to</u> an
explanation of the
refund policy**

再要一個購物袋
**<u>ask for</u> / <u>request</u>
another shopping
bag**

附有保固卡
**come with
a guarantee
card**

詢問／確認是否有保固
**<u>ask</u> / <u>check</u> if the
<u>warranty</u> / <u>guarantee</u> is
included**

SENTENCES TO USE

Piper 要求這名店員找小一點的裙子。
Piper asked the sales clerk to look for the dress in a smaller size.

我們到結帳櫃檯排隊等候吧。
Let's wait in line at the check-out counter.

若消費超過 200 美元的話，有些店有時候可以提供免運，所以也許你可以問一下店員是否可以運送。
Sometimes some stores deliver when you pay over $200, so you might want to ask the clerk if delivery is possible.

Finn 想先去拿到停車優惠，然後再要一個購物袋。
Finn wanted to get his parking validated before he could ask for another shopping bag.

你能查一下這個包包有沒有附保固卡嗎？
Can you check if this bag comes with a guarantee card?

上網購物
shop online

在／從…
（某網站）訂貨
order at / from ~

預購…（某商品）
pre-order ~; put ~ in a
pre-order request

比較物品／價格
compare goods /
prices

將…（某商品）放入購物車中
add ~ to one's shopping /
check-out list

將…加入願望清單中
add ~ to one's
wish list

使用折價券
apply a discount
coupon

支付運費
pay for delivery
/ shipping

輸入運送地址
enter one's
shipping address

使用安全／虛擬／臨時電話號碼
use a "safe number"
/ virtual number /
temporary phone
number

合併訂購（團購）
make a joint
purchase; put in a
joint order

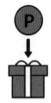

使用獎勵金／回饋點數
use bonus
/ reward points

SENTENCES TO USE

上次我上網購物時，不小心輸入了我以前的地址。
Last time I shopped online, I accidentally entered my previous address.

我已經收到我預購的最新款手機。
I received the latest mobile phone that I pre-ordered.

Jena 將她侄子的生日禮物添加到她的願望清單中，以便稍後做選擇。
Jena added her nephew's birthday gifts to her wishlist to choose later.

他對這個網路商城無法使用運費折抵券而感到憤怒。
He was mad at the online mall for not being able to apply a discount coupon for the shipping fee.

我總是使用虛擬號碼來送貨，以避免身分被盜。
I always use a virtual number for my shipping to avoid identity theft.

透過海外代購商購買物品
use / buy through an overseas purchasing agent

進行跨國購物
make a direct overseas purchase;
purchase overseas

PCCC?

輸入個人報關代碼
enter one's PCCC (personal customs clearance code)

查看訂單詳細內容
check the details of an order

查看物流追蹤資訊
check the tracking information

seller

向賣家提出問題
leave / post a question to the seller

Too slow!!!

向賣家抱怨延遲到貨
complain to the seller about delayed delivery

只收到部分訂貨
get / receive a partial shipment

將 A 換成 B
exchange A for B

退回…
return ~

寫評論並附上照片
post / write a review with a photo

SENTENCES TO USE

每次在海外網站購物時，我都得因延遲到貨向賣家抱怨貨品延遲送達。
Every time I purchase overseas, I have to complain to the seller about the delayed delivery.

如果您覺得自己誤訂了什麼，要去查看一下訂單明細。
You need to check the details of your order if you feel like you ordered something wrong.

請先查看物流追蹤資訊後，再向賣家提出送貨問題。
Please check the tracking information before leaving a delivery question to the seller.

Iris 收到一部分的聖誕訂購商品，且還在等待另一件包裹送達。
Iris received a partial shipment of her Christmas shopping and she is waiting for another package to arrive.

Susan 要求賣家將她有瑕疵的牛仔褲換成短裙。
Susan asked the seller to exchange her faulty jeans for a short skirt.

10

活動

ACTIVITIES

社交聚會

邀請…來參加社交聚會
invite ~ to a social <u>gathering</u> / <u>event</u> / <u>party</u>

加入一個開放式聊天團體
join an open chat group

參加股票投資會議
participate in a stock investment meeting

加入讀書會
join a study group

參加派對
attend a party

去參加品酒活動
go to a wine tasting

SENTENCES TO USE

去年我受邀參加一場社交活動，但我沒有去，因為我是一個內向的人。
I was invited to a social event last year, but I did not go because I am an introvert.

我在股票投資會議上獲得了一些很好的建議。
I received some great tips at the stock investment meeting.

加入當地一個小型的…團體
join a small local ~ group

辦一場社交聚會
form a social meeting / get-together

參加同學會
attend / go to one's school reunion;
go to an alumni reunion / meeting

交換電話號碼
exchange
(phone) numbers

與熟識的朋友一起去上烹飪課
go to a cooking class with close
acquaintances

享受下午茶聚會
enjoy a(n) (afternoon) tea party

Flora 昨天加入當地的一個保齡球團體，她喜歡這種氣氛。
Flora joined a local bowling group yesterday and she likes the atmosphere.

他去參加同學會是為了可以見到他的初戀情人。
He went to his school reunion to meet his first love.

Hannah 在享受茶會後與大家交換了電話號碼。
Hannah exchanged phone numbers with people after enjoying a tea party.

A 我從朋友那裡聽到過很多。很高
興見到你。
▶ I've heard a lot from my friend.
Nice to meet you.

B 真的嗎？我也很高興見到你。 你
看起來和照片有點不一樣！
● Really? Nice to meet you, too.
You look a little different from
the picture!

當然，是從好的方面來看。我想
你經常在做體能運動吧。
● In a good way, of course.
I guess you work out a lot.

A 謝謝。似乎是如此沒錯。
▶ Thank you. It might look like
that.

我自從拍了那張照片之後就一直
努力鍛鍊著。
▶ I've been working hard since I
took that picture.

從開始工作又生病之後，我一直
很照顧自己的健康。
▶ After getting a job and getting
sick, I am continuously taking
care of my health.

你喜歡運動嗎？
▶ Do you like to work out?

B 是的，我經常做瑜珈和皮拉提
斯。
● Yes, I do yoga and Pilates
constantly.

我還試著一個月去兩次健行。
● I'm also trying to go hiking
twice a month.

A 了解。健康是最重要的。
▶ I see. Health is the most
important thing.

下班後你通常會做什麼？
▶ What do you usually do after
work?

B 我去補習班學習義式美食烹飪，
也加入了一個讀書會。
● I learn Italian cooking at the
academy and also go to a book
club.

我們每個星期都會一起念書以及
評論書籍，以各種方式進行詮釋
是很有趣的事。
● We read and review books
together every week and it's fun
to interpret it in various ways.

你呢？
● What about you?

A 哇，聽起來你似乎是個大忙人！
▶ Wow, you sound like a busy person!

在平日時，我去參加游泳課程以及在健身房運動。
▶ During the week, I take swimming lessons and work out at the gym.

不久前，我還每天去參加一個一對一人體外貌拍攝的個人訓練課程。
▶ Not too long ago, I got one-on-one personal training every day to take a body profile picture.

週末時，我會在家休息或是去找朋友。
▶ On weekends, I rest at home or meet my friends.

我不喝酒，所以我通常會找好的餐廳而不是酒吧。
▶ I don't drink, so I usually look for good restaurants rather than bars.

B 那很好啊。我會去健行或者看電影 — 如果有什麼有趣的影片正在上映。
● That's amazing. I go hiking or watch movies if there is anything interesting.

A 了解。我經常和單車俱樂部的成員一起騎單車或是去健行。
▶ I see. I often ride a bicycle with my cycle club members or go hiking.

我也喜歡電影，所以我每個月會去看兩次電影。
▶ I also like movies, so I go to the movies twice a month.

下次我們一起去看電影吧？
▶ Shall we watch a movie together next time?

B 好啊！我希望我們可以一起看電影，然後一起去餐廳享用美食。
● Great! I hope we can watch a movie and eat delicious food at a restaurant.

我們也可以找一天一起去健行。
● We can hike together someday, too.

A 太好了。那我們來訂個日期吧。
▶ Very good. Then let's set a date.

2 電影院

查看電影的上映日期
check the release date
of the movie

尋找正在上映的電影
<u>look</u> / <u>search</u> for a movie that is currently
<u>showing</u> / <u>playing</u> / <u>screening</u>

查看電影票房排名
check the box office ranking

在售票亭購買電影票
buy a movie ticket at the box office

上網訂電影票
<u>book</u> / <u>reserve</u> a movie ticket online

指定／預訂座位
<u>designate</u> / <u>reserve</u> a seat

SENTENCES TO USE

Vince 在選擇一部電影之前一定會查看票房排名並觀看預告片。
Vince always checks the box office ranking and watches the preview before he
chooses a movie.

Sunny 對於沒有訂到最賣座電影的位子感到遺憾。
Sunny regretted on not reserving a seat for a top ranking movie.

買爆米花和飲料
buy popcorn and
drinks / beverages

將手機開靜音
set / put one's smartphone on
mute / silent / silent mode

觀賞電影預告片
watch a movie preview / trailer

觀賞一部電影
watch / enjoy a movie

看3D電影
watch a 3D movie

給予評分及寫評論
leave / write ratings and reviews

Daniel 總是自備零食，從不在電影院買爆米花或飲料。
Daniel always brings his own snack and never buys popcorn or drinks at movie theaters.

有一次看電影時，我忘了把手機設置為靜音模式，然後手機就響了！
One time, I forgot to set my phone on silent mode and it rang during a movie!

我總是在看完電影後給予評分和評論，因為我可以賺取積分。
I always leave ratings and reviews after I watch a movie because I can earn points.

觀賞戲劇／音樂劇
<u>watch</u> / <u>see</u> a <u>play</u> / musical

觀看街頭藝人表演
<u>watch</u> / <u>see</u> a <u>busking</u> / <u>street</u> performance

聽講座／座談會
listen to a <u>lecture</u> / <u>forum</u>

去逛展覽
go to an exhibition

手工製作陶藝
make pottery by hand

看一場⋯表演／比賽
watch a ~ <u>performance</u> / <u>contest</u>

SENTENCES TO USE

一對年輕夫婦站在路邊觀看街頭藝人表演。
A young couple stood by the road to watch a street performance.

我和女兒一起去看藝術展，並體驗製作明信片。
I went to an art exhibition with my daughter and experienced making a postcard.

Miranda 有手工製作陶藝的嗜好。
Miranda has a hobby of making pottery by hand.

你的家人喜歡看芭蕾舞表演嗎？
Does your family like watching a ballet performance?

在文化中心上…課程
take a ~ <u>class</u> / <u>lesson</u>
at a cultural center

朗誦詩歌
recite <u>a poem</u> / <u>poetry</u>;
read one's poetry aloud

體驗製作…
experience making ~

參加讀書俱樂部
participate in a <u>reading</u>
/ <u>book</u> club

參加社會服利／社區中心的花藝課程
take lessons in flower arrangement at
a <u>welfare</u> / <u>community</u> center

我祖母在文化中心上乒乓球課。
My grandmother takes a table tennis lesson at a cultural center.

我不敢相信 Sam 參加讀書俱樂部，還可以大聲朗讀他的詩歌。
I can't believe that Sam participates in a reading club and reads his poetry aloud.

去健身房／健身中心
go to the <u>gym</u>
/ <u>fitness center</u>

重新報名參加
re-register

報名加入健身中心
make a new registration at the gym;
get newly registered at the gym

穿上／換穿體育服
<u>put on</u> (=wear) / <u>change into</u>
one's sportswear

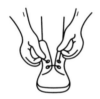

穿上運動鞋
put on (=wear) one's <u>sneakers</u>
/ <u>workout shoes</u>

接受運動諮詢
<u>get</u> / <u>receive</u>
exercise counseling

SENTENCES TO USE

她去健身房重新報名加入會員。
She went to the gym to re-register as a member.

Don 不知道他必須穿自己的運動鞋，因為他才加入。
Don did not know he had to wear his own sneakers because he just got newly registered.

在我們測量您的體脂肪之前，為什麼不換上運動服呢？
Why don't you change into your sportswear before we measure your body fat?

接受培訓員的指導
<u>be</u> / <u>get</u> coached by a trainer

測量體脂肪
measure one's body fat

開始運動前先做伸展（運動）
stretch before
<u>exercising</u> / <u>a workout</u>

上一對一私人課程
<u>take</u> / <u>have</u> a <u>one-on-one</u> /
<u>private</u> lesson

上小組課程
<u>take</u> / <u>have</u>
a <u>group</u> lesson

流汗後沖洗一下
<u>wash</u> / <u>clean</u> up after sweating

運動前的伸展動作應可預防受傷。
It is likely that stretching before exercise prevents injury.

如果您無法決定參加一對一或是小組課程，請先接受諮詢。
If you can't decide on taking a one-on-one lesson or a group lesson, get counseling first.

做有氧運動
do aerobic exercise;
do cardio (exercise)

在跑步機上跑步
run on a treadmill

做重量訓練
do weight training

舉啞鈴
lift dumbbells

做有氧舞蹈
do aerobics (dance)

在田徑場上步行／跑步
walk / run the track

做深蹲運動
do squats

進行武術訓練
train in martial arts

進行體能訓練
work on one's
physical strength

使用運動器材
use the exercise
equipment

深呼吸
take a deep
breath

進行最後總結的運動
do a finishing
exercise

上皮拉提斯訓練課程
get / take a
Pilates lesson

SENTENCES TO USE

讓我們以舉啞鈴的方式來做些簡單的重量訓練。
Let's do some easy weight training by lifting dumbbells.

下午有幾個女士團體在做有氧運動。
There are several lady groups doing aerobics in the afternoon.

在進行武術訓練之前，你得先進行體能訓練。
You need to work on your physical strength before you can train in martial arts.

使用運動器材之前請先閱讀説明。
Please read the instructions before using the exercise equipment.

在做深蹲時做深呼吸。
Take deep breathes in between squats.

C10U4_2.MP3

進行球類比賽
play ball games

參加田徑賽
take part in a track and field competition

加入／報名參加晨間足球俱樂部
join / sign up for a morning soccer club

參加（業餘）市民棒球聯盟
play in the citizens baseball league

經由決議而獲勝
win / score a decision; win by a decision

贏得全體一致通過的勝利
win by a unanimous vote / decision

以和局收場，不分勝負
play to a draw; result / end in a tie

犯規
commit a foul

被警告
get / receive a warning / yellow card

對於判決表示不服
complain / file a complaint about a judgment / ruling

被驅逐出場
be / get sent out of a game; get / receive a red card

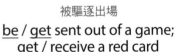

SENTENCES TO USE

能夠參加田徑比賽並獲得獎牌，我感到非常榮幸。
It's a great honor to take part in a track and field competition and win a medal.

這支當地的晨間足球俱樂部裡有許多中年男子。
There are a lot of middle-aged men in this local morning soccer club.

我男友每週六都在市民棒球聯盟出賽。
My boyfriend plays in the citizens baseball league every Saturday.

比賽中過度鬥毆可能會收到警告。
Excessive tussles in a match can lead to getting warnings.

犯規過多的運動員可能被驅逐出場。
Athletes who commit too many fouls can get sent out of a game.

（室內）攀岩
go (indoor)
rock climbing

騎越野自行車
ride a mountain bike

搭帳篷露營
pitch / set up / put up a tent and camp

在戶外烤肉
have an outdoor barbecue

去釣魚
go fishing

打高爾夫球；室內高爾夫球練習
play golf; play indoor golf / golf simulator

SENTENCES TO USE

現在很多人都去室內攀岩。
A lot of people go indoor rock climbing these days.

熱愛戶外活動的人也常喜歡去外面搭帳篷露營。
People who love outdoors also tend to like to pitch a tent and camp outside.

下水游泳或乘船釣魚前請穿上救生衣。
Please put on a life vest before swimming in water or go fishing on a boat.

去滑雪；從事滑雪板運動
go skiing / ski; go
snowboarding / snowboard

駕駛遊艇
sail a yacht /
cruise in a yacht

從事滑水運動
go water skiing

從事跳傘活動
go skydiving; skydive

從事滑翔翼活動
go paragliding; paraglide

騎馬活動
go horseback / horse riding

滑輪溜冰／內聯滑冰運動
go roller-skate / in-line skating

我等不及冬天可以去滑雪了！
I can't wait for the winter when I can go snowboarding!

膽大的人喜歡從事跳傘或滑翔翼等極限運動。
Daredevils love extreme sports like skydiving or paragliding.

11

自我管理

SELF MANAGEMENT

美容院

跟理容院約時間
make a reservation / an appointment
for a hair salon; make a hair appointment

穿上長袍
put on a gown

稍微修剪
get one's hair trimmed;
get a trim; trim one's hair

剪頭髮
have / get one's
hair cut; get a hair cut

將頭髮打薄
get one's hair thinned out;
thin out one's hair

用電動剃頭器修剪頭髮兩側
get one's sides shaved with a hair clipper;
shave one's sides with a hair clipper

燙頭髮
get a perm;
have one's hair permed

SENTENCES TO USE

那家髮廊太有名了，都預約不到。
That hair salon is so famous that it is impossible to make a reservation.

我們在燙髮之前先穿上這件長袍吧。
Let's put on this gown before getting a perm.

我不喜歡把頭髮剪得太短，所以修剪一下就好。
I don't like to get my hair cut too short, so I just get a trim.

C11U1.MP3

染髮
get one's hair died;
<u>dye</u> / <u>color</u> one's hair

將頭髮漂白
get one's hair bleached;
bleach one's hair

把頭髮吹乾
get one's hair blow-dried;
blow-dry one's hair

把頭髮盤起來
get one's hair put up, put one's hair up

將頭髮束起來
get one's hair tied; tie one's hair

用髮膠／髮蠟固定髮型
get one's hair fixed with hair <u>wax</u> / <u>gel</u>;
fix one's hair with hair <u>wax</u> / <u>gel</u>

把頭髮梳直
get one's hair straightened;
straighten one's hair

當她把頭髮漂白且試著要染髮時，她的大部分頭髮都脫落了。
Most of her hair fell off when she bleached her hair and tried to dye it.

空服員通常會將頭髮盤起來，並用髮膠固定。
Flight attendants usually put their hair up and fix it with hair gel.

C11U2.MP3

換穿按摩衣
change into
massage clothes

脫掉上衣／襯衫
take off one's
<u>top</u> / <u>shirt</u>

做足浴
take a foot bath

進行全身按摩
<u>get</u> / <u>receive</u> a
full-body massage

在身體上塗油
apply oil to one's
body

做芳香精油按摩
<u>get</u> / <u>receive</u> an
aroma oil massage

做足部按摩
<u>get</u> / <u>receive</u> a foot
<u>massage</u> / <u>footrub</u>

做經絡按摩
<u>get</u> / <u>receive</u> a
meridian massage

做頭皮按摩
<u>get</u> / <u>receive</u> a
scalp massage

背部做熱石按摩
put a massage
stone on one's back

燒香薰來放鬆
burn incense to
relax

SENTENCES TO USE

如果您脫掉上衣做按摩會害羞的話，請不要去按摩院。
If you are too shy to take off your top for a massage, please don't go to the massage parlor.

一邊泡腳一邊喝熱茶，非常放鬆。
Drinking hot tea while taking a foot bath is very relaxing.

我去越南或泰國時，喜歡享受芳香精油按摩。
I love getting aroma oil massages when I visit Vietnam or Thailand.

您想做乾式按摩還是油壓按摩？
Would you like a dry massage or an oil massage?

按摩師用香薰讓我感覺放鬆，但我不喜歡它的味道。
The masseuse burned incense to get me relaxed, but I don't like the scent of it.

3 美甲護理

C11U3.MP3

做美甲（藝術）護理
<u>have</u> / <u>get</u> one's nails done;
<u>have</u> / <u>get</u> a manicure

修腳趾甲
<u>have</u> / <u>get</u> a
pedicure

挑選指甲設計樣式
choose nail
designs

（在指甲上）塗指甲油
have gel
nails applied

清除膠甲
have gel nails removed;
<u>remove</u> / <u>take off</u> gel nails

在…貼上指甲貼
put nail stickers on ~

接受內生指甲的護理
have one's <u>fingernails</u> /
<u>toenails</u> cared for

去除腳上的死皮
get the dead skin
removed from one's feet

在…戴假指甲
put <u>fake</u> / <u>false</u>
nails on ~

處理內生腳趾甲
get ingrown toenails treated;
<u>take care of</u> / <u>treat</u> ingrown toenails

SENTENCES TO USE

對於有選擇困難的人來說，挑選指甲設計樣式並不容易。
Choosing a nail design isn't easy for people who have difficulty selecting.

清除膠甲相當費時。
Removing gel nails takes a long time.

大多數女性小時候都貼過指甲貼。
Most women have put nail stickers on their fingers as a girl.

別再咬指甲了！不然你之後得戴假指甲了。
Stop biting your nails! You are going to have to put fake nails on later.

現在有許多男士會去美甲沙龍店處理他們的內生腳趾甲。
A lot of men get their ingrown toenails treated at the nail salon nowadays.

卸妝
remove one's
makeup

進行基本皮膚護理
<u>put on</u> / <u>apply</u> basic skin care

去看皮膚科醫生
go to the dermatologist

臉部去角質
exfoliate one's face

分享個人的護膚秘訣／做法
share one's skincare <u>tips</u> / <u>routine</u>

擠壓粉刺或痘痘
<u>squeeze</u> / <u>pop</u> one's <u>pimple</u> / <u>acne</u>

SENTENCES TO USE

請務必在睡前卸妝。
Please make sure to remove your makeup before going to bed.

不要每天都做臉部去角質。那會讓你的皮膚變得更敏感。
Stop exfoliating your face every day. You're going to agitate your skin.

許多美容網紅分享她們有效的護膚心得。
Lots of beauty influencers share their effective skincare routines.

點痣
remove / take out a mole;
have a mole removed

做臉部按摩
get a facial massage

用面膜敷臉
apply / do a face / facial mask

冰敷⋯
apply / put an ice pack on ~

皮膚變得敏感
one's skin becomes
sensitive; agitate one's skin

做⋯（部位）的除毛
wax one's ~ hair;
get ~ hair removal

塗防曬乳液
wear sun cream
/ sunscreen / sunblock

Mia 去看皮膚科醫生時喜歡在那裡做臉部按摩。
Mia likes to get facial massages when she goes to the dermatologist.

將冰敷放在浮腫的眼睛上會減緩腫脹。
Putting an ice pack on your puffy eyes will decrease the swelling.

正在減肥，進行節食計畫
go / be on a diet

減重，減肥
lose weight

降低體脂
lose / reduce body fat

增加肌肉質量
gain / increase muscle mass

在家做運動
do an
at-home workout

接受飲食諮詢
receive / get (a) diet consulting

SENTENCES TO USE

隨著年齡增長，減重變得更加困難。
Going on a diet gets harder as one gets older.

在節食中減少體脂並增加肌肉質量是重要的。
It is important to lose body fat and gain muscle mass in a diet.

我和媽媽每天早上都會進行在家運動。
My mother and I do an at-home workout every morning.

制定一份飲食菜單
plan out a <u>diet menu</u> / <u>meal plan</u>

少量飲食
eat <u>little</u> / <u>light</u>; eat like a bird

訂購大量的雞胸肉
order a lot of chicken breast

攝取蛋白質奶昔
<u>take</u> / <u>eat</u> / <u>drink</u> a protein shake

查看體重變化
check one's weight change

我和我的飲食顧問一起制定了一份膳食計畫。
I planned out a meal plan with my diet consultant.

少量飲食並多運動是減重的關鍵。
Eating light and moving a lot is the key point in losing weight.

喝很多蛋白質奶昔並不會讓你長肌肉。你必須做運動！
Drinking lots of protein shakes does not give you muscle. You need to work out!

6 形象管理

參加形象諮詢（課）
<u>get</u> / <u>receive</u> image consulting

定期做臉部護理／皮膚療程
<u>get</u> / <u>receive</u> a <u>facial</u> / <u>skin treatment</u> regularly

做整形手術
<u>get</u> / <u>undergo</u> plastic surgery

接受肉毒桿菌素注射
get a Botox (injection)

將頭髮做個造型
get one's hair styled

上妝
put on makeup

SENTENCES TO USE

我會定期和媽媽一起到我的皮膚科醫生那裡做臉。
I regularly get a facial at my dermatologist with my mother.

一位氣象播報員在上節目之前化妝並將她的頭髮做了個造型。
A weather forecaster put on makeup and got her hair styled before she aired.

控制面部表情
control one's facial expression

對著鏡子做臉部表情的練習
practice one's facial expressions in the mirror

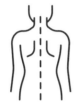

矯正姿勢／體態
have / get one's posture / body corrected

接受個人辨色診斷
get / receive a personal color diagnosis

接受聲音／發音矯正
have vocal / pronunciation correction

閱讀對話技巧方面的書籍
read a book about conversation skills

Chris 先生必須矯正他的姿勢，因為他一直都是低頭垂肩的樣子。
Mr. Chris needs to get his posture corrected because he is slouching all the time.

在接受個人辨色診斷之後，我發現我一直穿著不太適合我的衣服。
After getting a personal color diagnosis, I found out that I've been wearing clothes that don't look good on me.

如果你想增加自信，何不試著找一本有關對話技巧的書來看呢？
Why don't you try reading a book about conversation skills if you want to gain confidence?

在美加地區
維持良好形象應注意
的禮儀

在特定情境中，以適當的距離來交談。

在與美國或加拿大的母語人士交談時，有一個不成文的準則，那就是根據彼此親密度的不同，保持不同的交談距離。根據美國人類學家 Edward T. Hall 的研究，基於對話雙方的親密程度不同，有四種不同的談話距離標準。首先，在距離 45 公分以內的近距離交談，這是與家人、戀人等非常密切的關係的人的距離，被稱為「intimate space」。而距離 46 公分至 122 公分範圍稱為「personal space」，這是與親密的朋友，或是彼此已建立一定信任關係的朋友所保持的交談距離。在約 1.2 公尺至 3.6 公尺的距離範圍，被稱為「social space」，這是與一般認識的人的交談距離。而距離 3.7 公尺以上的範圍則稱為「public space」，這是與不特定對象進行交談的距離。總而言之，在美加地區，我們根據與對方的關係程度，保持適當的交談距離是基本的禮儀。在排隊時站得太近，或者日路時跟對方靠得太近，或者對陌生人進行輕微觸碰的行為，都可能給人留下非常失禮的印象，因此要特別注意。

握手時表現自信，交談時看著對方的眼睛

在商務場合中，初次見面時常有互相介紹、交換名片或者握手示好的情況。在美加地區，初次見面的標準握手方式

稱為「firm handshake」，即雙方應面帶自信，表情明亮，且注視對方的眼睛，用右手緊握對方的手，輕輕搖動一下。這種握手方式可展現你的自信和給人的信任感。然而，在國內許多場合，人們在握手時經常不會互相對視，而是用握住對方的手腕，或者僅僅輕輕握住對方手尖，這稱為「limp handshake」。在西方文化中，這樣的握手方式可能被誤解為缺乏自信，且讓對方感到不舒服或你在回避的態度，因此需要注意。在美加地區，彼此交談時也必須看著對方的眼睛，自信地進行交流。如果在對話中不敢與對方對視、低頭或看向其他地方，可能給人一種缺乏自信或不真誠的印象，這可能阻礙了良好關係的建立，不可不慎。

握住門把，等待下一位

一般來說，如果後面的人沒有立即跟上，通常不需要為了後面的人而握住門把等待。

然而，在美加地區，即使後面的人稍微遠一些，握住門把等待，或者當後面有多人時，由最前面打開門的人擋住門的關閉，等其他人進入，此舉被視為一種普遍的禮儀。相反地，當對方打開門等待你進入時，請輕聲說一聲 Thank you. 表示感謝。

當你要說「I am sorry」時，請表現出真心懊悔的表情。

當我們必須向對方表示歉意並說聲 I am sorry 時，應該用充滿真誠和懊悔的表情，並以展現出嚴肅的神情。在表達歉意時，如果表情過於冷漠或者在說出口時面露微笑，可能給人一種不真誠或嘲諷的印象，因此要格外小心。

A 如果我想讓自己更討人喜歡，我
該怎麼做呢？
▶ What should I do to look more
likable than I am now?

B 你得先改變一下髮型。
● You have to change your
hairstyle first.

半捲曲的長髮看起來很凌亂，也
難以整理。
● Semi-curly and long hair
can look messy and be hard to
manage.

以你的年齡來說，你的白髮多了
點，所以我認為你可以試試深棕
色系的短髮，應該會很適合你。
● You seem to have more gray
hair for your age, so I think you'll
look good in a short cut with a
dark brown color.

A 好的，那麼皮膚保養要怎麼做呢？
▶ Yes, how about my skincare?

B 由於你的皮膚偏乾，務必每隔兩
天用一次保濕面膜。
● Since your skin is dry, make
sure to use a moisturizing facial
mask every other day.

你的臉部除了黑頭之外，也必須
去角質。
● You should get your moles
removed from your face and
exfoliate.

我也建議你到 ABC 皮膚科嘗試
B型護膚，因為你有疤痕必須清
除。
● I also recommend you to
get skin care type B at ABC
dermatology because you need
to get scar removal.

A 知道了。那我的身材如何管理呢？
▶ Okay. How about managing
my body shape?

B 你的體重比你的標準體重多了 10
公斤。
● You are 10kg overweight to
your normal weight.

為了減少體脂肪並增加肌肉質
量，你必須同時集中有氧運動和
重量訓練。
● You need to reduce body fat
and increase muscle mass, so
you need to focus on aerobic
exercise and weight training at
the same time.

由於你的上半身相對於下半身來說肌肉較為不足,所以我們將進行下半身鍛鍊計畫。

● Your lower body muscles are weak compared to the upper body, so we are going to proceed with the lower body training program.

你的飲食計畫是最重要的,您應該按照我們提供的減重飲食方案進食,直到減重結束前,請避免攝取高鹽食物。

● Your diet is the most important thing. You should eat according to the diet we provide and you should not eat salty food until the end of the diet.

A 我擔心會出現溜溜球效應。

▶ I am worried about the yo-yo effect.

B 我們的中醫減重計畫有助於改善你的身體健康,因此,如果您繼續參與我們的計劃並做運動,你就不必擔心那件事。

● Our oriental diet program helps improve your physical health, so if you continue with our program and exercise, you won't have to worry about that.

我也建議你加入我們的姿勢矯正診所。

● I also recommend you to join our posture correction clinic.

A 太多了吧!似乎會讓我口袋大失血了!請您提供每一項課程的價格清單,並告知我即可。

▶ That's a lot! It seems like it would cost a lot, so please set up a list of the prices for each program and let me know.

CHAPTER

12

愛情

LOVE

相親 & 見面

向…（某人）介紹認識的人
introduce one's acquaintance to ~

安排一場相親
<u>set</u> / <u>fix</u> up on a blind date

去相親
go on a blind date

參加團體約會
have a group <u>meeting</u> / <u>date</u>

參與閃電約會
go speed <u>dating</u> / <u>date</u>

分享興趣愛好
share one's hobby

分享／談論共同的興趣
<u>share</u> / <u>talk about</u> a common interest

SENTENCES TO USE

所有我安排過的相親對象都成功步入婚姻。
All the couples I set up on a blind date succeeded in getting married.

在大學時和朋友一起參加閃電約會很有趣。
It's fun to go speed dating with friends in college.

Rowan 在和他的約會對象分享共同興趣和嗜好之後，已安排好下一次的約會。
Rowan planned for the next date after he and his date shared common interests and hobbies.

SORRY

禮貌性地拒絕／結束
decline / end
politely
/ respectfully

各自買單
pay one's bills separately; go Dutch;
split the check / bill

用餐後吃甜點
have a dessert
after a meal

聯絡牽線者並表示氣憤
call the middleman
/ go-between and get angry

彼此不適合
be not meant to be; be not
destined for each other

向…（某人）邀約第二次約會
ask ~ on / for
a second date

拒絕第二次約會
refuse to go on a second date;
turn down / decline a second date

如果約會對象不合你的心意，請禮貌性地拒絕，不要失禮。
If you don't like your date, please don't be rude and decline respectfully.

他不再發訊息給我了。我想我們彼此不來電。
He stopped texting me. I guess we weren't meant to be.

一見鍾情
be in love at
first sight

被愛情沖昏頭（神魂顛倒）
be blinded by love; fall head over heels

去約會
go on a date

對…有好感
have a <u>thing</u> / <u>feeling</u> for ~

曖昧中
have a fling

玩曖昧
play hard to get;
play games

（與…）四人約會
go on a double date (with);
double-date (with)

SENTENCES TO USE

雖然不是一見鍾情，但最終他還是盲目地陷入了愛河。
It was not love at first sight, but he was eventually blinded by love.

我年紀有點大了，不會玩曖昧，所以如果你對我有好感，就直接告訴我吧。
I am a little old to play hard to get, so if you like me, please just tell me.

那對情侶和另一對情侶出去約會，最終卻雙雙愛上另一對的伴侶。
That couple went on a double date, and ended up falling in love with the other couple's partners.

C12U2.MP3

告白；約某人出去
confess one's <u>feelings</u> / <u>love</u>;
ask someone out

（與⋯）交往；（與⋯）談戀愛
go out (with); have a (romantic)
relationship (with)

寫情書
write a love letter

約定下次約會
<u>set</u> / <u>plan for</u> a next date

真心真意地送花
<u>present</u> / <u>give</u> flowers with all one's heart

談網戀
date online

Troy 已開始和約會 app 上認識那個的女生交往。
Troy started going out with the girl he met on a dating app.

當我們還在曖昧階段時，他就經常寫情書給我，還送我禮物。
He used to write me love letters and give me gifts when we were having a fling.

C12U3.MP3

安排／籌備求婚事宜
<u>arrange</u> / <u>prepare</u> a
proposal event

準備訂婚戒指
prepare an
engagement ring

預約求婚地點
reserve a place for
one's proposal

向朋友尋求協助
ask one's friends
for help

（打電話）呼叫心愛的人
call in one's
lover

裝作沒事發生
act as if nothing had
happened; play innocent

營造浪漫氣氛
create a romantic
atmosphere

向戀人求婚
propose to
one's lover

求婚成功
succeed in
proposing

親吻戀人
kiss one's
lover

拒絕（某人的）求婚
turn down one's
(marriage) proposal

對於預料之外的失敗
感到尷尬
be embarrassed by
the shock of failure

SENTENCES TO USE

他打理好整個活動之後，竟然忘記預約他的求婚地點。
He arranged a whole event and then forgot to reserve a place for his proposal.

如果你認為自己無法獨力完成，不妨向朋友們尋求幫助。
If you don't think you can do it yourself, ask your friends for help.

製造浪漫氛圍，並讓一切看似毫無心機，但卻是求婚成功的關鍵。
Creating a romantic atmosphere and playing innocent is a key to success in proposing.

Katie 在她男友接受她的求婚後親吻了他。
Katie kissed her boyfriend after he said yes to her proposal.

有誰能想到 Diana 會拒絕 Ralph 的求婚呢？
Who would have thought that Diana would turn down Ralph's proposal?

4 吵架 & 分手

C12U4.MP3

情侶爭吵
have a lover's quarrel

（分手後）復合，
舊情復燃
get back together

對…不忠
cheat on ~

劈腿被抓到
be / get caught cheating

與…搞外遇
have an affair with ~;
play / fool around with ~

表達心情的不悅（失望）
express one's disappointment

和…分手
break / split up with ~

被甩了
be / get dumped / dropped

拋棄…（某人）
dump / drop ~

封鎖某人的電話號碼
block one's phone number

刪除合拍的照片
delete the pictures taken together

保留／珍惜回憶
keep / cherish / treasure one's memory

解除婚約
break off one's engagement / wedding

離婚
get divorced; get a divorce

SENTENCES TO USE

許多情侶在說出心裡的話之後，便舊情復燃了。
Many couples get back together after talking things out.

Melissa 在和情侶爭吵之後表示相當失望。
Melissa expressed her disappointment after a lover's quarrel.

我知道是我拋棄了他，但我仍珍惜我們的回憶！
I know I dumped him, but I still cherish our memories!

Harry 被抓到和前女友搞外遇後就被拋棄了。
Harry got dumped after he was caught cheating with his ex-girlfriend.

分手後我一直封鎖前男友的電話號碼。
I always block my ex-boyfriend's phone number after I split up.

C12U5_1.MP3

安排準新人雙方家屬會面
<u>have</u> / <u>arrange</u> a meeting
between the families of
the couple to be wed

去新郎／新娘家拜訪
visit the <u>groom's</u> /
<u>bride's</u> house

向…提親；向…求婚
ask one's <u>permission</u> / <u>blessing</u>
for marriage; ask for the hand of ~

諮詢婚禮策劃師
consult a
wedding planner

簽訂婚宴地點的合約
make a contract with
a wedding <u>hall</u> / <u>venue</u>

拍婚紗
take one's
wedding photos

試穿婚紗／禮服
try on a <u>wedding
dress</u> / <u>tuxedo</u>

租借婚紗／禮服
rent a <u>wedding
dress</u> / <u>tuxedo</u>

選擇／決定蜜月地點
<u>choose</u> / <u>decide on</u> a
honeymoon destination

發送喜帖
<u>send</u> / <u>give</u> out
wedding invitations

安排新娘秘書化妝
<u>receive</u> / <u>get</u>
bridal makeup

SENTENCES TO USE

他去她家請求她的父母允許他們結婚。
He went to her house to ask her parents' permission for their marriage.

透過婚禮策劃師來簽訂一份婚宴場地合約可以省時省錢。
Making a wedding hall contract through a wedding planner can save time and money.

她為了租借一件漂亮的禮服來拍婚紗，正在進行著嚴謹的飲食計畫。
She was on a harsh diet to rent a beautiful dress for her wedding photos.

很多情侶在選擇蜜月地點時都會有爭執。
A lot of couples fight when they are trying to decide on a honeymoon destination.

見到朋友來發喜帖時總是一件令人驚訝的事。
It's always surprising to meet a friend when they are giving out wedding invitations.

結婚
get married; settle down;
tie the knot; get hitched

包禮金
pay / give
congratulatory
money

舉行小型婚禮
have a small /
garden / house
wedding

舉行傳統結婚式
have a traditional
wedding

聆聽主禮師致詞
listen to the
officiating speech

扔花球
throw
a bouquet

舉辦結婚儀式
host a wedding
ceremony

在婚禮上唱祝福歌
sing at / for
a wedding

交換結婚誓詞
exchange wedding
/ marriage vows

與賓客合影
take pictures with
the guests

參加婚宴
attend / go to
a reception

去度蜜月
go on
a honeymoon

SENTENCES TO USE

辦小型婚禮並享受豪華蜜月是目前的一種趨勢。
Having a small wedding and going on a luxury honeymoon is a trend nowadays.

如果不要辦傳統結婚式，你可以節省婚禮的預算。
You can save on wedding budget by taking out the traditional wedding ceremony.

一位著名的歌手在我姐的婚禮上獻唱。
A famous singer sang at my sister's wedding.

我們省去主禮師致詞的部分，僅進行交換結婚誓詞，讓這場結婚式更加精簡。
Let's keep the wedding concise by exchanging wedding vows without the officiating speech.

新人通常在婚宴結束後開始蜜月旅行。
A couple usually goes on their honeymoon after the reception ends.

A 親愛的，既然我們都見過雙方父母了，且也敲定結婚日了，我們就開始計畫婚禮吧。
▶ Babe, since we met each other's parents and decided on a date, let's start planning for our wedding.

我朋友（之前）透過婚禮策劃師來籌備婚禮，一切她都很滿意。
▶ My friend prepared everything through a wedding planner and loved everything about it.

B 你是說最近新婚的 Hannah 嗎？
● You mean Hannah who got married recently?

她的婚紗照拍得很美，婚宴禮服和妝容也相當時尚且漂亮。
● Her wedding photos came out pretty. The wedding dress and the makeup were stylish and pretty as well.

我們也該考慮找她的策劃師諮詢一下嗎？
● Should we consult with her planner too?

A 好啊。婚禮場地呢？
▶ Good. What about the wedding venue?

價格差異很大，從平價的普通場所到豪華飯店宴會聽都有。
▶ The price difference is huge from cost-effective regular venues to luxury hotel venues.

B 要不要像我們之前討論過的，只邀請家人和親近的朋友辦一場小型婚禮？我另一位好友就在蒙特綠灣的度假小屋辦婚禮。我只想像那樣只邀請少數人，然後辦一場派對式的婚禮。
● How about having a small wedding with family and close friends like we talked before? My other best friend got married at a pension in Montgreen Bay. I want to only invite a small number of people like that and have a wedding with a party.

A 好啊，那我們也考慮小型婚禮吧。
▶ Okay, let's take small weddings into consideration.

你想好要去哪裡度蜜月了嗎？
▶ Have you thought about the honeymoon destination?

B 我覺得馬爾地夫可能是最好的選擇。
● I think the Maldives is the best.

在海灘度假的一個星期，可以游泳又可以按摩，這樣很棒。
● It would be nice to go swimming and get massages at the beach for about a week.

你覺得呢？
● How about you?

A 嗯…其實我想去歐洲之類的地方，可以觀光、品嚐美食、欣賞美麗的夜景，以及參與各種活動。
▶ Hmm… Actually, I want to go to places like Europe and go sightseeing, eat delicious food, see the great night view, and do various activities.

B 我想要我們的蜜月是個兩人世界的旅行，不受任何人的打擾。
● I want our honeymoon to be just the two of us without other people's interference.

你不這麼認為嗎？
● Don't you think so?

A 馬爾地夫費用有點貴且對於沙灘按摩來説也有點遠。
▶ The Maldives seems to be a little expensive and far away for beach massages.

我們何不找一個更近且價格較實惠的地方呢？
▶ Why don't we look for a place that is closer and more affordable?

B 那麼，我們就再多考慮一下。
● Then, let's give it some more thought.

下個月有一場婚宴博覽會，我們何不去那裡做個諮詢。
● There is a wedding fair next month, so why don't we get a consultation over there?

A 這是個好主意！
▶ That'd be great!

在比較過婚禮策劃師的提案與估價之後，再做決定會比較好。
▶ It would be good to decide after comparing wedding fair consultation and estimates by the wedding planner.

13

活動

EVENTS

策劃活動
<u>organize</u> / <u>plan</u> an event

預訂派對場地
reserve a party room

準備花束／蛋糕／禮物
prepare a <u>bouquet</u> / <u>cake</u> / <u>gift</u>

舉辦一場驚喜活動／派對
<u>have</u> / <u>hold</u> a surprise
<u>event</u> / <u>party</u>

邀請…（某人）參加派對
invite ~ to
the party

參加派對
attend
a party

聘請外燴業者；點外燴餐點
hire a buffet caterer;
call a caterer

準備短片
prepare
a short video

祝賀某人的紀念日／生日
celebrate one's
<u>anniversary</u> / <u>birthday</u>

拍攝紀念照
take a commemorative
photo

與…（某人）乾杯
make a toast
with ~

SENTENCES TO USE

他已將慶祝結婚紀念日的花束和鑽戒準備好了。
He prepared a bouquet and a diamond ring for his wedding anniversary.

哇！Lucia 邀請知名網紅參加她的生日派對！
Wow! Lucia invited famous influencers to her birthday party!

派對策劃師將大部分預算花在聘請飯店外燴業者。
The party planner spent most of the budget on hiring a hotel buffet caterer.

我準備了一段要在派對上展示的祝賀短片。
I prepared a short congratulatory video that I want to show at the party.

我們拿起香檳，為這對可愛的夫妻舉杯祝賀吧！
Let's make a toast with our champagne glasses for this lovely couple!

舉辦滿周歲慶祝宴
have one's first birthday party

贈送金戒指
give a gold ring as a present

觀看寶寶成長影片
watch a baby's growth video

玩滿月抓周
do a one-year-old catch

贈與／接受回禮
give out / receive a return gift

舉辦成人禮
hold a coming-of-age ceremony

慶祝六十／七十／八十大壽
celebrate one's 60th / 70th / 80th birthday

邀請某人的家人／朋友
invite one's family / friends

通宵跳舞玩樂
dance and enjoy all night

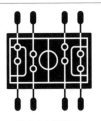

進行派對遊戲
play party games

與人們交際娛樂
hang out / socialize with people

SENTENCES TO USE

我在我姪女的滿月宴上送了個金戒指作為生日禮物。
I gave a gold ring as a present for my niece at her first birthday party.

何不送些獨特的回禮，而不是像毛巾那樣無聊的禮物？
Why don't you give out unique return gifts not boring gifts like towels?

Jamie 去年舉辦了她的成年禮。
Jamie held her coming-of-age ceremony last year.

為了祝賀祖母的八十大壽，父親請來了一位廣受歡迎的歌手。
My father hired a popular singer for my grandmother's 80th birthday celebration.

我在20多歲的時候曾經和朋友玩派對遊戲並通宵跳舞。
I used to play party games and dance all night with my friends during my 20s.

邀請參加生日派對
invite to one's birthday party

送生日禮物
give a birthday present

回覆參加派對的意願
RSVP to a party;
reply one's attendance
of a party

訂製蛋糕
customize /
custom-make a cake

在蛋糕上插上蠟燭
put / stick candles on a cake

點蠟燭
light a candle

SENTENCES TO USE

哎呀！我忘了回覆這週六參加他生日派對的意願。
Oops! I forgot to RSVP to his party this Saturday.

我的侄女想要一個獨特的訂製獨角獸造型生日蛋糕。
My niece wanted a custom-made unicorn shaped cake for her birthday.

唱生日快樂歌
sing a 'Happy Birthday' song

吹蠟燭
blow out
a candle

開玩笑地將鮮奶油塗在某人臉上
put whipped cream on
one's face for fun

開香檳慶祝
pop the champagne

在生日派對中盡情玩樂
enjoy one's birthday party

我們點蠟燭之後來唱生日快樂歌。
Let's sing a 'Happy Birthday' song after lighting the candles.

我真不敢相信我們玩笑地將鮮奶油弄在 Luna 臉上時讓她氣瘋了！
I can't believe Luna got mad for putting whipped cream on her face for fun!

我會忘記昨天發生的事情，並在明天 Tony 生日派對上盡情地玩。
I am going to forget what happened yesterday and enjoy Tony's birthday party tomorrow.

隨侍在終時者旁
watch over one's
<u>passing</u> / <u>death</u>

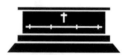

與殯儀館簽約
<u>make</u> / <u>sign</u> a contract with
a funeral home

確定墓地位置
decide on a burial
ground

撰寫訃聞通知
write an obituary
notice

發送訃聞訊息
send an obituary
message

發佈訃聞
publish an
obituary

準備往生者遺照
prepare a portrait
of the deceased

設置靈堂
set up a <u>mortuary</u>
/ <u>funeral parlor</u>

準備喪服
prepare mourning
(clothes)

為慰問者準備食物
prepare food for
<u>condolers</u> / <u>mourners</u>

SENTENCES TO USE

許多人在看著心愛的人離世後會有創傷症候群。
Many people get traumatized after watching over their loved one's passing.

與殯儀館簽約是一個人往生後要做的第一件事情。
Signing a contract with a funeral home is the first thing one should do after someone passes.

你能否幫我寫一份訃聞通知？我正忙著安排靈堂。
Could you write an obituary notice for me? I am busy setting up the funeral parlor.

以前人們習慣在報紙上發佈訃聞。
People used to publish an obituary on newspapers.

天啊，我沒有時間準備喪服。
Oh no, I don't have time to prepare mourning.

4 喪禮進行

C13U4.MP3

| 穿上喪服
wear mourning
(clothes) | 接待慰問者
accept / welcome
condolers / mourners | 舉辦紀念儀式
hold a memorial
service / ceremony | 焚香／供奉香燭
burn / offer
incense |

| 向故人獻花
lay flowers for the
deceased | 舉行蓋棺儀式
hold a coffin rite
ceremony | 移送至火葬場／墓地
move / go to the
crematorium / burial site |

| 依故人遺願進行火葬
cremate as the will
/ wish of the deceased | 將骨灰安置在骨灰堂
place one's remains / ashes
in the charnel house | 撒骨灰
scatter one's
remains / ashes | 為逝者下葬
bury the
deceased |

SENTENCES TO USE

在紀念儀式中點香是常見的事。
It is normal to burn incense at the memorial service.

我們家有向逝者獻花的傳統。
There is a tradition of laying flowers for the deceased in my family.

我們一起到墓地去，為逝者進行安葬。
Let's go to the burial site together and bury the deceased.

她的骨灰被安置在骨灰堂。
Her remains are placed in the charnel house.

Jane 按照父親的遺願將其骨灰撒在海灘上。
Jane scattered her father's ashes at the beach as he wished.

收到訃聞訊息
receive an obituary message

發送慰問訊息
send a message of consolation

送花圈至靈堂
send a wreath to the mortuary

繫上黑色領帶
wear a black tie

穿上黑色西裝
wear a black suit

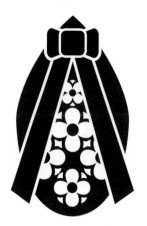

前往殯儀館
go to / visit a funeral home

SENTENCES TO USE

我一收到一位朋友的訃聞就立刻送花圈到靈堂。
I sent a wreath to the mortuary as soon as I received an obituary message from a friend.

通常男性到殯儀館穿著黑色西裝並繫上黑色領帶。
Men usually wear a black suit and a tie to a funeral home.

因為我必須到殯儀館去，所以要取消今天的約定。
I need to cancel our appointment today because I need to go to a funeral home.

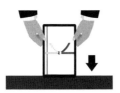

獻上白包
<u>pay</u> / <u>give</u> condolence money

（在逝者遺照前）默哀致意
<u>pay</u> / <u>offer</u> a silent <u>prayer</u> / <u>tribute</u>
(to the portrait of the deceased)

哀悼逝者
mourn for the deceased

在殯儀館吃腳尾飯
dine at a funeral home

慰問喪家
comfort one's bereaved family

一般通常白包要包多少呢？
How much do people usually give for condolence money?

我們一起默哀致意，然後過去慰問一下喪家。
Let's pay a silent tribute and go comfort the bereaved.

A　謹向故人致以深切的哀悼之意。
▶ I am sorry for your loss.

B　感謝您遠道而來致上慰問之意。
● Thank you for coming all this way to pay your respects.

A　我看他最近還是很健康。怎麼突然間發生了這樣的事？
▶ I thought he was healthy until recently. What happened all of a sudden?

B　由於年事已高，他經常有一些小病痛，但突然間他的肺炎惡化，不幸離世了。
● He has been getting sick frequently due to his age, but his pneumonia suddenly got worse before his passing.

不過，我很高興他臨終時所有家人隨侍在旁且留下遺言。
● Still, I was glad that he was able to leave his will and pass on with all his family by his side.

A　他今年 91 歲了，是吧？
▶ He was 91 this year, right?

我相信家人隨侍在旁時，他能夠安詳地離開。
▶ I'm sure he was able to move on comfortably with his family by his side.

安喪地點已經確定了嗎？
▶ Have you decided on a burial site?

B　是的，喪禮預計進行三天，我們會迎接前來慰問者，直到後天，然後前往火葬場。
● Yes, it's a 3-day funeral so we will accept condolers until the day after tomorrow and go to the crematorium.

火化後，骨灰將安置在紀念公園的陵寢。
● The remains will be placed in the burial chamber in the memorial park after cremation.

A 原來如此。我想您一定相當悲傷。但願他一路好走。
▶ I see. I'm sure you are grieving. I hope you can send him well.

我們父母本來打算跟我一起來，但因身體不適，所以我也代替他們致上慰問金。
▶ My parents wanted to come with me, but they weren't feeling well so I brought their condolence money as well.

B 對於他們送至靈堂的花圈及慰問金，我在此表達感恩。
● I am so grateful for their wreath sent to the mortuary and condolence money.

您已表示慰藉之意，麻煩前往餐廳用餐。
● Since you offered your prayers, please go to the diner and have dinner.

A 好的，我會過去。非常感謝。
▶ Yes, I will do so. Thank you very much.

14

回家之後

AFTER COMING
BACK HOME

回家

查看郵件信箱
check one's mailbox

按電梯的樓層按鈕
press a floor button on the elevator

搭乘電梯上樓
take the elevator up

回到家
return / come /
get back home

輸入門鎖密碼
enter the door lock password

SENTENCES TO USE

我總是會查看郵件信箱後再去搭電梯。
I always check my mailbox before getting on the elevator.

我現在還在一樓，因為我忘了按電梯的樓層按鈕！
I'm still on the first floor because I forgot to press my floor button on the elevator!

在你輸入門鎖密碼時，請用手掩蓋，以免被他人看見。
Please cover your hand when you enter the door lock password so no one can see.

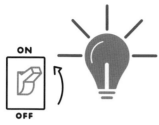

打開家裡的燈
turn on the lights in the house

放下包包
put down one's bag; set one's bag down

脫下衣服並放進洗衣機裡
take off one's clothes and put
them in the washing machine

換上居家衣服
change into indoor clothes

穿上室內拖鞋
wear indoor slippers

我不喜歡黑暗，所以回到家時會把家裡的燈都打開。
I turn on all the lights in the house when I get home because I don't like the dark.

你應該穿上室內拖鞋，以避免鄰居投訴聲音太吵。
You should wear indoor slippers to prevent noise complaints from neighbors.

2 晚餐

從冰箱中取出食材
take the ingredients <u>out of</u> / <u>from</u>
the refrigerator

（沖）洗水果／蔬菜
rinse <u>fruits</u> / <u>vegetables</u>
in water

用氣炸鍋烹飪
cook in an air fryer;
use an air fryer to cook

用平底鍋煎肉／煎魚
grill <u>meat</u> / <u>fish</u>
in a frying pan

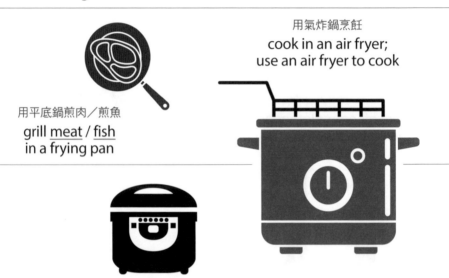

用電鍋蒸飯
use a rice cooker to cook rice

SENTENCES TO USE

你可以把冰箱裡的沙拉食材拿出來，然後用清水洗一下嗎？
Can you take out the ingredients for salad from the refrigerator and rinse them in water?

自從開始使用氣炸鍋煮東西，準備晚餐變得更加輕鬆了。
Preparing dinner became easier since I started to use an air fryer to cook.

我們現在都用電鍋煮飯，但我奶奶以前習慣用普通的鍋子煮。
We use a rice cooker to cook rice now, but my grandmother used to cook rice in regular pots.

做一道菜
make a dish

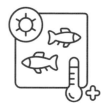

將冷凍食品解凍
thaw frozen food

吃晚餐
<u>have</u> / <u>eat</u> dinner

吃第二碗飯
<u>have</u> / <u>eat</u> a second helping

叫外送
order food by delivery

吃宵夜
take / <u>have</u> a late-night <u>snack</u> / meal

因為 Erin 不想煮飯，她訂了中國菜的外送。
Erin ordered Chinese food by delivery because she didn't want to cook.

昨天晚上我們宵夜吃義大利麵。
We had spaghetti for a late-night snack yesterday.

A　喂，親愛的，你今天忙嗎？
▶ Hey, honey. Were you busy today?

B　嗯，早上去了一趟客戶那，然後回公司開始寫報告，還要準備明天的業務簡報。所以，我不得不加班。
● Yup, I went to a client in the morning, returned to work, wrote a report and had to prepare for tomorrow's business briefing. So, I couldn't help but work overtime.

你今天如何？
● How was your day?

A　今天店裡客人太多了，我忙翻了。
▶ I was so busy because there were so many customers at the store today.

所有員工都得接待客人，且急忙聯絡休假的兼差人員回來幫忙，但我們還是欠缺人手。
▶ All the employees responded to the guests and urgently contacted the off-duty part-timer for help, but we were still short-handed.

我很高興客人能夠體諒並耐心等候，要不然我可能就要收到很多投訴了。
▶ I was glad that the customers were considerate enough to wait, or else I would have gotten a lot of complaints.

B　因為你處理得很好，所以一切順利運作。
● It went well without problems because you did a great job.

你老板不該給你一點獎勵嗎？
● Shouldn't your boss give you a bonus?

A　呵呵。但願如此，但我不知道我老闆是否知道我如此辛苦地撐了過去。
▶ Ha. I hope so, but I don't know if my boss knows that I'm going through a hard time like this.

這個週末我們要做什麼呢？
▶ What shall we do this weekend?

B 我們何不找個風景優美的地方露營、放空一下,享受無所事事的悠閒,因為很久沒這樣了?
● Why don't we go camping in a beautiful place, zone out and have some down time since it's been a while?

A 那也不錯,但目前有很多好看的電影上映,要不要去看場電影,然後在外面吃一頓?
▶ That's good too, but since there are a lot of interesting movies released. How about going to the movies and eating out?

去露營還要搭帳篷,在戶外住宿是一種負擔,因為我的身體太疲憊了。
▶ It's going to be a burden to go camping, set up a tent, and stay outdoors because my body is so tired.

B 好的,那我們就這樣安排吧。
● Okay, let's do that.

啊!這週六還有一場棒球比賽,所以我們可以先看個早場電影,接著吃一頓美味的午餐,然後開車兜風、看球賽,最後享受炸雞和啤酒。
● Ah! There is a baseball game this Saturday, so we can watch a movie early in the morning, have a good lunch, go for a drive, go to the game and have chicken and beer.

A 這似乎是非常好的主意。
▶ That seems like a lovely idea.

棒球比賽結束後,我們可以去公園散步一下再回家。
▶ After the baseball game, let's take a walk in the park and go home.

B 好的!這週六就這樣安排,然後星期天在家好好休息。
● Great! Let's hang out like that on Saturday and rest at home on Sunday.

C14U3.MP3

打開電視
turn on
the TV

切換電視頻道
change TV
channels

調高／調低音量
turn <u>up</u> / <u>down</u>
the volume

查看電視節目列表
<u>look</u> / <u>skim</u> / <u>run</u> through the
TV <u>schedule</u> / <u>program listings</u>

看新聞／連續劇／廣告
watch the <u>news</u> /
<u>dramas</u> / <u>commercials</u>

看重播節目
watch a rerun
of a program

看有線電視頻道的電影
watch a movie on
cable TV

看單選付費節目頻道
watch a pay-per-view
channel

訂閱 VOD/OTT（隨選視訊／過頂）服務
subscribe to <u>VOD (Video-on-Demand)</u>
/ an <u>OTT (Over-the-Top)</u> media service

購買家庭購物頻道的商品
buy goods on a home
shopping channel

開啟字幕
turn on the
<u>caption</u> / <u>subtitle</u>

SENTENCES TO USE

我忘了這個遊戲節目的播放時間。你能幫我看一下電視節目表嗎？
I forgot when the game show is on. Can you skim through the TV schedule for me?

我通常用平板電腦看戲劇，以及看電視播的新聞。
I usually watch dramas on my tablet and watch the news on TV.

如果你還沒看過那部戲，一定要看一下重播。
You definitely have to watch the rerun of that drama if you have not seen it.

現今人們更傾向訂閱 OTT 媒體服務，而不是觀看一次性的付費頻道。
People nowadays subscribe to an OTT media service rather than watching a pay-per-view channel.

在看有線電視的電影時，一般來說都會開啟字幕。
It's typical to turn on the caption when watching a movie on cable TV.

4 電腦 & 網際網路

C14U4.MP3

登入／登出某個網站
log in to / out of
a website

將電腦開機
turn on the
computer

以使用者 ID 和密碼登入
use one's user ID and
password to log in

移動滑鼠並點擊
move the mouse
to click

在某入口網站上搜尋…
search (for) ~
on a portal site

使用鍵盤輸入文字
write / type on a keyboard

瀏覽網際網路
surf / browse the Internet

連接到 Wi-Fi
connect to a Wi-Fi

撰寫／發送電子郵件
write / send an email

回覆電子郵件
reply to an email

SENTENCES TO USE

如果你無法記住要登入的使用者帳號和密碼，把它寫在某處吧。
If you can't remember your user ID and password to log in, write it down somewhere.

你在去購物之前，最好先上網搜尋目前的潮流趨勢。
You better search current trends online before you go shopping.

為什麼在這隧道裡要連上 Wi-Fi 這麼難呢？
Why is it so hard to connect to a Wi-Fi in this tunnel?

我不用電腦上網，因為要連上 Wi-Fi 很困難。
I don't use my computer for surfing the Internet because it is difficult to connect to a Wi-Fi.

你能查看一下我們發給你的郵件並儘快回覆嗎？
Could you check the email we sent you and reply to it as soon as possible?

C14U5.MP3

輸入解鎖手機的圖案
enter a pattern
to unlock one's phone

打電話／接電話
make / take a
phone call

進行通話
talk on one's phone

撥打視訊電話
make a video call

使用表情符號發送文字訊息
send a text message
using emojis / emoticons

發送照片／影片
send a photo /
video

更新／備份手機資料
update / back up
one's phone

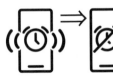

更改手機設定
change the settings
on one's phone

下載並使用應用程式
download and use an
app (application)

連接藍牙
connect to the
Bluetooth

將手機螢幕投射到電視螢幕上
mirror one's cell phone
screen to a TV screen

SENTENCES TO USE

設定指紋解鎖手機，免得你忘了解鎖手機的圖案。
Set up your fingerprint to unlock your phone just in case you forget the pattern to unlock your phone.

過去她常用文字簡訊發給她男友許多愛的表情符號。
She used to send a lot of heart emojis in her text messages to her boyfriend.

糟糕，我的手機壞了，而且我應該沒有做備份！
Oh no, my phone broke and I don't think I backed it up!

請將你們的手機關機，或者更改手機設定，以免在課堂上發出聲響。
Please turn off your phones or change the settings on your phone so that it does not ring during the class.

如果你想用更大的螢幕看，何不將手機畫面投射到電視螢幕上呢？
Why don't you mirror your cell phone screen to the TV screen if you want a bigger screen?

6 遊戲

C14U6.MP3

進入遊戲（程式中）
access / connect
to a game

玩電腦遊戲／線上遊戲
play a PC game /
an online game

完成任務後獲得獎勵
be rewarded for
completing the mission

參與一項活動
participate / take part
in an event

new
item!

RANK

創造角色
make / create
a character

獲得道具
obtain an
item

用現金購買道具
buy items with real cash;
pay for items in cash

提升…等級
level up ~

查看排名
check one's
ranking

與…的對戰開始
a matchup begins
/ starts with ~

加入一個聯盟／家族
join a league /
clan / party

與其他玩家比賽
play games with
other players

與其他玩家聊天
chat with
other players

SENTENCES TO USE

我完成了這場聖誕活動的任務，並獲得了獎勵。
I was rewarded for completing the mission during the Christmas event.

哇噢！我在與其他玩家參加的襲擊遊戲中獲得了一個稀有的道具！
Wow! I obtained a rare item when I participated in a raid with other players!

有很多孩子在父母不知情之下用現金買東西後就惹來一堆麻煩。
There are a lot of kids who get in trouble buying items with cash behind their parent's back.

一場家族對戰將於一週後開始。
A clan matchup will begin in a week.

為了體驗遊戲的順暢度，我們建議加入一個聯盟。
In order to experience a smooth flow of the game, we recommend joining a league.

C14U7.MP3

建立個人 SNS 帳戶
<u>create</u> / <u>make</u>
one's SNS account

訂閱／追蹤⋯的 SNS 頻道
<u>subscribe to</u> / <u>follow</u>
one's SNS channel

瀏覽貼文
look through
one's posts

對該內容按讚
click 'like' on the
content

在⋯上面留言
<u>post</u> / <u>write</u> a
comment on ~

在⋯上面留負評
<u>post</u> / <u>write</u> hateful
comments on ~

分享貼文
share one's post

在 SNS 帳戶上發佈貼文
upload a post
on one's SNS

發送／接收私訊
<u>send</u> / <u>get</u> a DM
(direct message)

封鎖⋯（某人）的帳戶
block one's
account

參加 SNS 上面的活動
participate in
an event on SNS

在 SNS 上發佈／上傳贊助產品
<u>post</u> / <u>upload</u> sponsored
products on one's SNS

SENTENCES TO USE

我五年前創建我的SNS帳戶，現在我是一位擁有大量粉絲的網紅。
I created my SNS account 5 years ago, and now I am an influencer with lots of followers.

每次我訂閱我孩子們的SNS時，我都會被封鎖在他們的帳戶外。
Every time I subscribe to my children's SNS, I get blocked from their accounts.

我平常會在空閒時瀏覽朋友的SNS並寫下評論。
I look through my friend's SNS and write comments in my free time.

Jenna 經常收到陌生人發來奇怪的私訊。
Jenna gets inappropriate DMs from strangers a lot.

知名網紅會在他們的SNS上發佈贊助產品而撈一筆錢。
Famous influencers get paid a lot for uploading sponsored products on their SNS.

8 結束一天

C14U8.MP3

將摺好的衣物收進櫃子裡
put the folded laundry
in the drawer

修剪手指甲／腳指甲
trim one's <u>nails</u> /
<u>toenails</u>

使用按摩椅／按摩器做按摩
massage with a <u>massage
chair</u> / <u>massager</u>

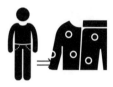

換上睡衣
change into
one's pajamas

打電話給情人／
朋友／家人
call one's <u>lover</u> /
<u>friend</u> / <u>family</u>

查看明天的行程
check tomorrow's
schedule

躺在床上用手機上網
lie down and use the
Internet on one's smartphone

設置鬧鐘
set an alarm

將手機接上充電器
plug one's cell phone
into a charger

ON

OFF

關掉房間的燈
turn off the light
in one's room

上床睡覺
go to bed

SENTENCES TO USE

下班後回到家坐在按摩椅上按摩是一天完美的結束。
Massaging with a massage chair at home after work is the perfect end of the day.

換上睡衣後，我打算打電話給我朋友。
I am going to call my friend after I change into my pajamas.

我習慣躺下來後用手機查看明天的行程。
I have a habit of lying down and checking tomorrow's schedule on my smartphone.

他因為沒有設置鬧鐘而考試遲到了。
He was late for an exam because he didn't set his alarm clock.

睡覺前不要忘記將手機接上充電器！
Don't forget to plug your cell phone into a charger before you go to bed!

15

週末 & 假日

WEEKEND & HOLIDAYS

露營 & 野餐

C15U1.MP3

將食物打包放進保冷箱
**pack food
in an ice box**

準備露營裝備
**pack one's camping
equipment**

收拾帳篷／遮陽篷
**clear a <u>tent</u> /
<u>shade</u>**

搭起帳篷／遮陽篷
**set up a <u>tent</u> /
<u>shade</u>**

在陰涼處鋪上墊子
**<u>spread</u> / <u>lay</u> a mat
in the shade**

在溪邊戲水
**play in the water
by the stream**

將手提燈點亮
**turn on a
portable lantern**

將即食品加熱
**heat up precooked
<u>foods</u> / <u>meals</u>**

燒木炭
**set charcoal on fire;
fire up the charcoal**

燒木炭來烤肉
**<u>barbecue</u> / <u>grill meat</u>
on charcoal**

圍著營火坐下
**sit around a
<u>campfire</u> / <u>bonfire</u>**

清理營地
**clean up one's
campsite**

SENTENCES TO USE

從他搭帳篷的方式可以看出他是個新手。
You can tell that he is a newbie by looking at the way he sets up a tent.

為什麼我們不在陰涼處鋪上墊子，然後讓孩子們去戲水呢？
Why don't we lay the mat in the shade and let the kids play in the water?

你可以將手提燈點亮，然後燒木炭生火嗎？
Can you turn on the lantern and fire up the charcoal?

來吧！我們圍著篝火坐下，烤些棉花糖吧。
Come on! Let's sit around the bonfire and roast some marshmallows.

我討厭人們在收拾帳篷後沒有清理他們的營地。
I hate it when people don't clean up their campsites after clearing the tents.

2 外出

C15U2.MP3

準備好簡單的食物和飲料
**pack simple food
and drinks**

在城市的郊區呼吸新鮮空氣
**get some fresh air <u>outside</u>
/ <u>at the outskirts of</u> the city**

在一個景點開車兜風
**take a drive
in a scenic spot**

欣賞周圍的景觀
**look around the
landscape**

呼吸新鮮的空氣
breathe in fresh air

購買博物館／展覽館／植物園的門票
**get a ticket to <u>a museum</u> / <u>an
exhibition hall</u> / <u>an arboretum</u>**

獲取導覽手冊
get a brochure

聆聽導覽員的解說
**listen to the guide's
explanation**

與…合照
**take a snapshot
with ~**

來個自拍
take a selfie

SENTENCES TO USE

我買了一輛車，可以每個週末到郊區去呼吸新鮮的空氣。
I bought a car to get some fresh air outside the city every weekend.

我和男朋友在郊區一個景點開車兜風。
My boyfriend and I took a drive in a scenic spot on the outskirts.

偶爾呼吸新鮮空氣是很重要的。
It is important to breathe in fresh air once in a while.

假日期間的展覽館門票不容易買得到。
It is hard to get tickets to an exhibition during holidays.

我通常都用自拍，因為沒有人幫我拍照。
I usually take a selfie because no one takes a photo for me.

A 今天的棒球比賽太精彩了，是不是？
▶ That was a great baseball game today, right?

B 一點都沒錯！在九局兩出局的情況下，有誰能想到打者會擊出逆轉勝的滿貫全壘打呢？
● Totally! Who would have imagined that the batter would hit a grand slam to win a losing game with two outs in the ninth inning?

我原以為我們球隊會以 2:5 輸掉比賽，後來卻以 6:5 贏了，真是令人興奮得無法靜下來。
● I thought our team would lose 5 to 2, but I am still so hyped after winning 6 to 5.

A 可以理解。
▶ I know.

我看見敵隊的加油觀眾席上，所有人都啞口無言且神情呆滯。
▶ When I looked at the opponent's cheering section, everyone was speechless and lost their minds.

B 他們一定震驚得說不出話，畢竟他們以為是贏定了。
● They must have been dumbstruck, since they thought they won.

A 現在比賽結束了，我們該做些什麼呢？
▶ What should we do now that the game is over?

B 我們去吃點東西吧。你可以上網看一下這附近有什麼好吃的嗎？
● Let's eat something. Can you look for a good place around here on the Internet?

A 嗯，離這裡地鐵站約 300 公尺有一家有名的豬排餐廳。
▶ Hmm. There is a famous pork cutlet restaurant near the subway station 300 meters away from here.

這家電視報導過好幾次，評價非常好。價格也不貴。
▶ It was on TV several times and the reviews are really good. It's inexpensive, too.

B 真的嗎？太好了。我們先去那裡吃豬排，然後到詹姆斯江公園散散步吧。

● Really? That's good. Let's eat pork cutlets there and go for a walk in James River Park.

A 我查了一下，從詹姆斯江公園入口往南走約 2 公里處可以搭詹姆斯江遊輪。

▶ I looked it up and there is a place where we can take the James River cruise 2 kilometers south of the James River Park entrance.

我們去坐看看如何？

▶ Why don't we try that?

B 真是個好主意。不過兩公里有點遠，我們還是騎自行車過去吧。

● That's a great idea. It's a little far if it is 2 kilometers, so let's take a bike.

A 好的。我們搭遊輪過去的話，河的對岸有一家景觀優美的咖啡廳。

▶ Sure. If we take the cruise ship and get off the other side of the river, there is a cafe with a good view.

我們可以在那裡喝咖啡，同時欣賞日落。

▶ Let's drink coffee there and enjoy the sunset.

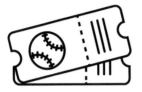

取得／購買比賽門票
<u>get</u> / <u>buy</u> a
ticket to a game

帶上加油工具
pack one's cheering gear

前往球場／比賽現場
go to the <u>stadium</u> / <u>game</u>

和應援團一起呼喊口號
chant with the cheering squad

觀賞啦啦隊的表演
watch a cheerleader
performance

查看電子顯示器上的比賽／選手資訊
check the <u>game</u> / <u>player</u> information
on the electronic display

SENTENCES TO USE

如果你忘記帶應援裝備，我們就得玩波浪舞為他們加油。
If you forgot to pack your cheering gear, we are going to have to cheer by doing the waves.

在觀賞啦啦隊表演時，請保持一些尊重。
Please show some respect when you are watching a cheerleader performance.

因為有一位新球員加入，我們得查看一下電子顯示幕上的球員資訊。
We need to check the player information on the electronic display because there is a new player.

C15U3.MP3

向敵隊的一方發出噓聲
<u>boo</u> / <u>jeer</u> one's opposing team

對選手的失誤／受傷感到遺憾
be sorry for the player's <u>mistake</u> / <u>injury</u>

得分時鼓掌叫好
applaud for scoring

玩波浪舞表示歡呼
cheer by doing the waves

為獲勝的選手歡呼
cheer for the victorious players

為失利的選手加油
cheer up the defeated players

發出噓聲以及干擾敵隊，是沒有運動家精神的行為。
Booing and interrupting the opposing team is not very sportsmanlike.

重要的是要鼓勵被擊敗的隊伍，而不是戲弄他們。
It is important to cheer up the defeated team instead of teasing them.

上網搜尋美食餐廳
search for <u>must-eat</u> / <u>good</u>
restaurants on the Internet

RESERVED

預訂外食地點
reserve a place to eat

將名字列入等候名單
put one's name on the waiting list

點菜
choose a <u>menu</u> / <u>dish</u>

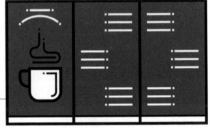

向服務員詢問熱門餐點
ask the server about the popular menu

點餐
order a meal

SENTENCES TO USE

糟糕！我忘記訂位了，所以我們只好列入等候名單了。
Darn it! I forgot to reserve a table, so we have to put our name on the waiting list.

如果你無法決定點什麼，何不請服務生推薦一下熱門佳餚呢？
If you can't decide what to order, why not ask the server about the popular menu?

C15U4.MP3

再加點一些食物
order <u>more</u> / <u>extra</u> food

詢問我湯匙／叉子／筷子放哪
ask for <u>a spoon</u> / <u>a fork</u> / <u>chopsticks</u>

與家人／朋友一起享用美食
enjoy a meal with one's <u>family</u> / <u>friend</u>

請結帳（準備買單）
ask for the bill

將剩餘的食物打包
pack the leftovers

對食物的味道提出投訴
complain about the taste of food

我妹妹上網找到這家餐廳，且我們喜歡這裡全部的餐點。
My sister found this restaurant on the Internet, and we enjoyed the whole meal.

我們請了帳單，並分開結帳。
We asked for the bill and split the check.

我打算將剩下的食物包回家給我的狗吃。
I am going to pack my leftover for my dog at home.

C15U5.MP3

將空調／暖氣轉強一些
crank up the <u>air conditioner</u> / <u>heating</u>

從室內欣賞外面的天氣
enjoy the weather from indoors

用預備好的餐包烹飪
cook with meal kits

（勉強地）用…將就一下
make do with ~

將便飯放入微波爐加熱
microwave <u>instant</u> / <u>pre-cooked</u> rice

發呆
<u>space</u> / <u>zone</u> out

與家人交流
have a conversation with one's family

做些喜歡做的事
<u>have</u> / <u>pursue</u> a hobby

處理（堆疊的）待洗衣物
do one's (piled-up) laundry behind schedule

趕進度看電視劇集（追劇）
<u>catch up on</u> / <u>binge-watch</u> TV dramas

閱讀書籍
read a book

SENTENCES TO USE

我喜歡把冷氣調強一些，然後蓋著我這條鬆軟的毯子。
I love to crank up the AC and get under my fluffy blanket.

現在獨居的人很流行用預備好的餐包來烹飪。
It is a current trend for one-person households to cook with meal kits.

我們就用上次午餐的剩菜將就一下吧。
Let's just make do with leftovers from last lunch.

我不想做任何事情，只想躺在床上發呆。
I don't like to do anything but space out on my bed.

Theresa 週末不和我們見面，因為她要一次追劇追個夠。
Theresa is not meeting us on the weekend because she needs to binge-watch her dramas.

6 宗教

C15U6.MP3

信仰（某宗教）
believe in

前往教堂／天主教堂／寺廟
go to <u>church</u> / <u>Catholic</u>
<u>church</u> / <u>Buddhist temple</u>

改信⋯
convert to ~

（還）沒有宗教信仰
have no religion (yet)

是個無神論者
be an atheist

對他宗排外
<u>exclude</u> / <u>reject</u> other religions

包容他宗
<u>embrace</u> / <u>tolerate</u>
other religions

踏上朝聖之路
go on a
pilgrimage

被邪教纏身
<u>get into</u> / <u>fall for</u> a <u>pseudo-</u>
<u>religion</u> / <u>cult</u>

SENTENCES TO USE

我母親原本是天主教徒，但她10年前皈依佛教了。
My mother was a Catholic but she converted to Buddhism 10 years ago.

我沒有宗教信仰不代表我是無神論者。
Not having a religion does not mean that I am an atheist.

有些宗教要求信徒踏上朝聖之旅。
Several religions require believers to go on a pilgrimage.

你聽說過他所有家人加入一個邪教，然後某一天都消失了嗎？
Did you hear that his whole family got into a cult and vanished one day?

參與一場禮拜
attend a service

參加教會活動
attend church

5:30 AM

參加清晨的禮拜
attend an early morning service

2:00 AM

舉行一場通宵禮拜
hold an all-night service

參加一場線上祈禱儀式
attend an online worship service

唱讚美詩
sing a hymn / songs of praise

（盡）奉獻（義務）
give / make an offering

聽講道
listen to the sermon

十一奉獻
give tithes; tithe

傳教
evangelize

閱讀／抄寫聖經
read / transcribe the Bible

參與聖經研讀；加入聖經學習小組
study the Bible; participate in a Bible study group

Christianity

上浸禮班課程
take a baptism class

SENTENCES TO USE

我祖父母過去習慣每週一參加清晨的禮拜。
My grandparents used to attend an early morning service every Monday.

由於無法抗拒的情況，本週的禮拜將在線上舉行。
Due to unavoidable circumstances, worship service will be held online this week.

我哥哥曾是在教堂唱讚美詩歌的詩班少年。
My brother was a choirboy singing hymns at church.

他在聽講道時睡著了。
He fell asleep while listening to the sermon.

我出國留學時曾加入一個聖經研讀小組。
I participated in a Bible study group when I was studying abroad.

去參加教會培靈會
go to a church retreat

參加復興會
attend a revival
(meeting)

到禱告所祈禱
go to the house
of prayer to pray

作見證
give a
testimony

在復活節前進行 40 天的禁食
fast for 40 days
ahead of Easter

教主日學；擔任主日學老師
teach Sunday school; become
a Sunday school teacher

被任命為（女）執事/長老
be appointed
deacon (ess) / elder

得到牧師的祝福
get blessed by
a pastor

背誦主禱文／使徒信經
recite the Lord's Prayer
/ Apostles' Creed

閱讀教會週報通告
read a weekly
church news / report

站在教會詩班中
stand in one's
church choir

SENTENCES TO USE

我曾經喜歡參加教會的培靈會。
I used to like going to a church retreat.

我母親過去曾一連數週去禱告所禱告，所以我和我的兄弟姐妹們一點也不喜歡。
My mother used to go to the house of prayer to pray for weeks at a time, so my siblings and I didn't like it at all.

Daniel 一直想要成為青少年主日學的老師。
Daniel always wanted to become a Sunday school teacher for the youth.

我的阿姨被任命為我們教會的新女性執事。
My aunt was appointed as the new deaconess of our church.

Debra 站在她教會的詩班中，盡情地唱出她的心聲。
Debra stood in her church choir and sang her heart out.

宗教活動 – 天主教

去參加一場彌撒
go to mass

進行一場復活節／聖誕節彌撒
give <u>an Easter</u> / <u>a Christmas</u> Mass

參加線上彌撒
attend mass online

唸頌玫瑰經禱告
pray the rosary

聆聽講道
listen to the sermon

做十字聖號敬拜聖體
cross oneself

佩戴面紗
wear a veil

（幼兒）接受受洗
**be baptized
(as a baby)**

領受受洗之名
**be christened ~ ;
get a baptismal name**

去告解
**<u>go to</u> / <u>make a</u> confession;
confess (one's sins)**

參與靈修聚會
**<u>take</u> / <u>receive</u>
communion**

SENTENCES TO USE

他手上拿著誦經用念珠聽著講道。
He listened to the sermon with a rosary in his hands.

她在祈禱時做了個十字聖號。
She crossed herself when she was praying.

婦女在祈禱時佩戴面紗是一種習慣。
It is customary for women to wear veils when they pray.

Selena 還是個嬰兒時就受洗了。
Selena was baptized as a baby.

你多久必須去一次告解？
How often do you have to go to confession?

進行靈修活動
go on a (religious) retreat

成為疏遠信仰的天主教徒
become a lapsed Catholic

舉行禱告聚會
hold a prayer
meeting

成為某人的教母／教父
become one's godmother /
godfather

背誦禱告文
recite a prayer

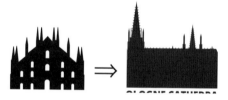

參與不同的教會活動
move from church to church

SENTENCES TO USE

Luna 在她父親過世後成了一名疏遠信仰的天主教徒。
Luna became a lapsed Catholic after her father passed away.

我最好的朋友請我擔任她女兒的教父。
My best friend asked me to become her daughter's godfather.

9 宗教活動 – 佛教

參加佛教法會
attend a
Buddhist service

向佛祈願；在佛寺內敬拜
pray to Buddha;
offer a Buddhist prayer;
worship in the Buddhist temple

合掌拜佛
put one's hands together
<u>in front of the chest</u>
/ <u>as if in prayer</u>

轉動念珠（進行祈念）
count one's beads

（發出聲音）讀經
read the Buddhist
scriptures (out loud)

虔誠敬拜
make a deep bow

進行一百零八次敬拜
make one hundred
and eight bows

燒香
burn incense

懸掛蓮花燈籠
<u>hang</u> / <u>put</u> up a lotus lantern

點燃蓮花燈籠／蠟燭
light a <u>lotus lantern</u> / <u>candle</u>

SENTENCES TO USE

每年有一場慶祝佛陀誕辰日的佛教儀式，會有數千人參加。
There is an annual Buddhist service with thousands of people on the Day of Buddha's Coming.

僧侶大聲地讀誦佛經。
The monks read the Buddhist scriptures out loud.

每天進行一百零八次敬拜已讓我的膝蓋軟骨磨損了。
I've worn out my knee cartilage by making 108 bows every day.

我喜歡在寺廟裡聆聽木魚的聲音並聞著香火的味道。
I like the sound of wooden fish and the smell of burning incense at the temple.

我母親為我們全家人點燃了一盞蓮花燈籠。
My mother lit a lotus lantern for our whole family.

出家當和尚
become a
Buddhist monk

敲打木魚
beat / tap / knock on
a wooden fish

修行
practice
asceticism

參禪修行
do Zen meditation;
do zazen

參加寺院住宿體驗
participate in /
join temple stay

進行繞塔儀式
circle the pagoda

接受法名
get / receive one's
Buddhist name

理解輪迴（或轉世）思想
understand the concept
of reincarnation / rebirth

聆聽佛教講座
listen to the monk's
sermon

捐獻
give alms; donate / offer
money / rice

SENTENCES TO USE

他在很小的時候就出家了。
He became a Buddhist monk at an early age.

許多外國人喜歡參加寺院住宿體驗。
A lot of foreigners like to participate in temple stay.

她很榮幸能夠從僧侶那裡得到她的法名。
She was honored to get her Buddhist name from the monk.

信徒要理解輪迴的概念並不容易。
It is not easy for believers to understand the concept of reincarnation.

佛教信徒總是慷慨捐獻，例如捐贈米飯和水果。
Buddhist devotees always give alms such as rice and fruits.

16

旅行

TRAVEL

旅行準備

擬定旅行計劃
plan a trip; <u>make</u> / <u>come up with</u> a travel plan

設定旅行預算
figure out one's travel budget

選定旅行地點
<u>choose</u> / <u>decide on</u>
a <u>place</u> / <u>location</u> to travel;
decide on one's travel destination

規劃旅行路線
set a course for one's trip

確認護照有效日期
check the expiration date of
one's passport

SENTENCES TO USE

在你選擇旅行地點之前先確定好旅行預算，這似乎是明智之舉。
It seems wise to figure out your travel budget before you decide on a location to travel.

我無法相信你居然沒檢查你護照的有效日期！
I can't believe you didn't check the expiration date of your passport!

拍護照／簽證用的照片
take a <u>passport</u> / <u>visa</u> picture

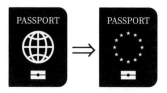

換發護照
get one's passport reissued

取得簽證
get a visa

換發國際駕照
get one's international driver's license issued

購買旅行保險
take out travel insurance

接受必要的預防接種
get mandatory vaccinations

你可以輕鬆地上網申請並取得簽證。
You can easily apply online and get a visa.

如果你預計會在國外租車，別忘了先換發國際駕照。
Don't forget to get your international driver's license issued if you are planning on renting a car overseas.

幸運的是，Sue 有買旅行保險，且在旅途中她的手機損壞後得到了賠償。
Fortunately, Sue took out travel insurance and got compensation for her broken cellphone during her travel.

訂前往⋯的機票／火車票
book a <u>flight</u> /
<u>train</u> ticket to ~

預訂飯店／度假村／旅舍／民宿
book / <u>reserve</u> a <u>hotel</u> / <u>resort</u> /
<u>hostel</u> / <u>B&B</u>

準備機票／文件的影本
make copies of <u>tickets</u> /
<u>documents</u>

查看當地天氣
check the local weather

打包行李
pack up one's travel luggage

SENTENCES TO USE

Kate 想要訂一張飛往馬德里的機票，但已經沒有座位了。
Kate wanted to book a flight ticket to Madrid, but there were no seats left.

先上網查看當地天氣狀況，再來打包行李。
Check the local weather on the Internet and pack clothes accordingly.

準備好急救藥品／處方藥／維他命
pack <u>first-aid medicine</u> / <u>prescription</u>
<u>medicine (drugs)</u> / <u>vitamins</u>

C16U1_2.MP3

準備旅行用變壓器
pack a travel adapter

整理旅行用品和化妝品樣品
pack up travel supplies and
cosmetics samples

1234 4567 8901 2345

辦理信用卡
get a credit card issued

趁手續費較低時換鈔
exchange money when
the commission is low

再次確認所有預訂
<u>confirm</u> / <u>recheck</u> all
reservations

如果你在出國時需要將手機充電，別忘了帶旅行用變壓器！
Don't forget to pack a travel adapter if you want to charge your phone overseas!

Amber 為了旅行特地保留了很多化妝品樣品。
Amber saved a lot of cosmetics samples for her travels.

我辦了這張信用卡，因為它的國際交易手續費最低。
I got this credit card issued because its foreign transaction fee is the lowest.

我習慣去機場前重新檢查所有的預訂。
I have a habit of rechecking all reservations before I leave for the airport.

A 親愛的，這次假期要去哪玩，你有任何想法了嗎？

▶ Darling, have you given any thoughts about where to go for this vacation?

B 是的，因為我們去過峇里島很多次了，這次就去別的地方如何？

● Yes, since we've been to Bali a lot, how about we go to other places this time?

A 嗯，我想你的護照今年就要到期了。你的護照還在有效日期內嗎？

▶ Hmm, I thought your passport expires this year. Is the expiration date okay?

B 還好。我還有 8 個多月才到期。出國旅遊應該是沒問題的。

● It's fine. I still have 8 more months until expiration. There should be no problem traveling overseas.

A 來一趟泰國的跟團行程如何？還是要自由行？

▶ How about a package tour to Thailand? Or a self-planned trip?

B 我們跟團去泰國已經好幾次了，所以來一趟關島自由行怎麼樣？

● We have been on a package tour to Thailand a few times, so how about a self-planned trip to Guam?

A 好啊，但因為跟團有很多優惠，可能比自由行還便宜，且我們不必分別預訂機票和飯店。

▶ Okay, but due to lots of discounts, package tours can be cheaper than self-planned trips where we need to book flights and hotels separately.

現在跟團有很好的選擇，還有自由的時間。

▶ There are good options and free times for package tours nowadays.

B 但跟團也沒得選擇只能在購物中心購物之類的不是嗎？

● But don't package tours have mandatory shopping time at the malls and stuff?

C16U1_PU.MP3

A 是這樣沒錯，但我想我們還是可以很快地四處晃晃，在購物中心裡吃點東西然後按摩一下之類的。
▶ That's true, but I think we can just have a quick look, eat something and get a massage inside the shopping mall or something.

B 現在離度假的時間不多了，還要查這查那的似乎挺麻煩的。
● There is not much time left until vacation, and it seems inconvenient to look into this and that.

我們還是去跟團旅行吧！
● Let's go with the package tour.

選擇提供全套早餐選項的飯店會比較好。
● It would be better to choose the hotel with the full breakfast package option.

A 太好了！我之前保存了很多免稅店的優惠券，這次去關島的時候就可以用來買需要的東西了。
▶ Awesome! I have a lot of duty-free discount coupons saved up which I will use at the duty-free shops on our way to Guam and buy things that I need.

B 我也是！我的香水差不多用完了，到時候也會在免稅店買一些。
● Me, too! I am out of perfume, so I should buy it at the duty-free.

那麼，你能找一下去關島的旅行團嗎？
● Then can you look for the package tour for Guam?

我想我們可以在出發前一起買個旅遊險。
● I think we can take out travel insurance together before we go.

在機場登機櫃台辦理登機手續
check in at the airport check-in counter

接受／通過安全檢查
<u>get</u> / <u>pass</u> through a security check

登機
<u>board</u> / <u>get on</u> a plane

等候轉機
wait for one's connecting flight

接受入境審查（準備通關）
go through immigration

回答移民官的問題
answer the immigration officer's questions

SENTENCES TO USE

我喜歡在機場登機櫃台辦理登機手續以及寄送行李的感覺。
I love the feeling of checking in at the airport check-in counter and sending my baggage.

我們等轉機等了超過 4 個小時。
We waited over 4 hours for our connecting flight.

我想移民官員花了幾個小時問我問題是因為他的問題我都答錯了！
I guess the immigration officer questioned me for hours because I answered his questions wrong!

C16U2.MP3

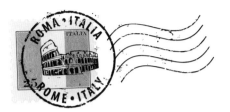

在護照上蓋章
get one's passport stamped

過海關
<u>go</u> / <u>pass</u> through customs

被海關攔查
be caught in customs

在行李認領區取回行李
pick up one's luggage at
the baggage claim

搭乘住宿接駁巴士
take a shuttle to one's
accommodation

Eugene 因為超過免稅額度而被海關攔查。
Eugene was caught in customs because he went over his duty-free limit.

在行李認領區取回行李後，你可以搭乘接駁車到達你的住宿地。
You can take a shuttle to your accommodation after picking up your luggage at the baggage claim.

3 免稅店 & 當地購物

購買紀念品
<u>purchase</u> / <u>buy</u> souvenirs

逛免稅店
look around duty-free shops

在機場免稅店購買…
<u>purchase</u> / <u>buy</u> ~ at the duty-free shop at the airport

購買免稅酒
<u>purchase</u> / <u>buy</u> duty-free liquor

以便宜價格購買名牌商品
<u>purchase</u> / <u>buy</u> luxury goods at a low price

SENTENCES TO USE

我已經有好一段時間沒逛免稅店了！
It has been a while since I looked around duty-free shops!

她男朋友買了幾瓶免稅酒。
Her boyfriend purchased a few bottles of duty-free liquor.

我很幸運能以便宜價格買到這個高檔名牌包。
I was lucky to be able to buy this luxury brand wallet at a low price.

使用免稅店折扣券
use duty-free discount coupons

查看免稅限額
check the duty-free limit

領取網購免稅商品
pick up duty-free goods purchased online

購買只有當地才買得到的東西
buy goods that can only
be purchased locally

購買…（某人）託買的物品
purchase / buy a requested item;
buy something that ~ asked for

拿到我在網路上買的免稅化妝品真是令人興奮。
It's exciting to pick up duty-free cosmetics I purchased online.

我在百貨公司買了一罐我妹妹託我買的面霜。
I bought a face cream that my sister asked for at the department store.

結帳離開…
check out of ~

登記入住…
check into ~

向飯店工作人員詢問旅遊資訊
ask the hotel staff for travel information

利用飯店提供的免費服務
take advantage of hotel
complimentary services

取得與飯店合作的旅遊景點優惠
get a discount on tourist attractions
affiliated to one's hotel

叫客房服務
order room service

SENTENCES TO USE

我向飯店工作人員詢問旅遊資訊時，他跟我說有一些旅遊景點的優惠。
When I asked the hotel staff for travel information, he told me about a discount on tourist attractions.

我的姪女未經父母許可就叫了客房服務，結果惹上了麻煩。
My niece got into trouble for ordering room service without her parent's permission.

享用自助早餐
have / eat a breakfast buffet

使用飯店游泳池
use the hotel swimming pool

與…（某人）一同享受飯店假期
enjoy a hotel vacation / staycation with ~

在 Spa 區做按摩
get a massage at a spa

欣賞海景／山景
enjoy the sea / mountain view

利用接駁車服務
use a shuttle service

我們到飯店游泳池的時候就開始下雨了。
It started to rain when we were at the hotel swimming pool.

上週末我跟朋友一同享受飯店假期。
I enjoyed a hotel staycation with my friends last weekend.

她喜歡在 Spa 區做按摩時欣賞海景。
She likes to enjoy the sea view while getting a massage at the spa.

踏上…（某地）之旅
go on a trip to ~; travel to ~

one-day trip

前往…（某地）進行一日遊
go on a one-day trip to ~

去自助旅行
go backpacking;
go on a backpacking trip

參加導覽旅遊
take part in a
guided tour

參加跟團旅行
go on a package tour

進行國內旅行
make / go on a
domestic trip

SENTENCES TO USE

我計畫今年夏天和家人一起去倫敦旅行。
I'm planning to go on a trip to London with my family this summer.

我寧願去自由行，也不要參加跟團旅行。
I'd rather go on a backpacking trip than go on a package tour.

出國旅遊
travel abroad

去環遊世界
travel around the world

進行國內跨界徒步旅行
go on a cross-country walking trip

踏上郵輪之旅／（出錢）讓…（某人）享受郵輪之旅
go on a cruise / send ~ on a cruise

去逛夜市
go to the night market

多數人都夢想著退休後能去環遊世界。
Most people have a dream of traveling around the world after they retire.

我在20出頭歲時曾在國內進行跨界徒步旅行，那是我最棒的經歷。
I went on a cross-country walking trip in my early 20s and it was the best experience I had.

我祖父母出錢讓我搭上郵輪之旅，作為我的畢業禮物。
My grandparents sent me on a cruise for my graduation gift.

我們一起去逛夜市吧！我聽說那裡很好玩。
Let's go visit the night market! I heard it's fun.

參觀／前往旅遊景點
visit / go to a tourist attraction

享受觀光樂趣
enjoy sightseeing

拍…（某人或物）的照片
take a photo of ~;
photograph ~

去當地餐廳用餐
visit / go to local restaurants

品嚐當地美食
try local food

體驗當地文化
experience the local culture

欣賞…的夜景
enjoy the night view of ~

SENTENCES TO USE

拍攝著名的旅遊景點是令人興奮的事。
It's exciting to take a photo of famous tourist attractions.

我在旅途中總是會去品嚐當地特色及稀有的美食。
I always try local exotic and rare food when I travel.

他們登上這棟摩天大樓欣賞城市夜景。
They went up the skyscraper to enjoy the night view of the city.

結束旅行歸來
come back from one's trip

在社交媒體（SNS）上分享旅行照片和心得
post pictures and reviews of the trip
on SNS

製作旅行相簿
make a travel
photo album

將旅行經歷說給…（某人）聽
talk to ~ about one's
travel experience

我在旅行期間絕不會忘記在社交媒體上發布照片。
I never forget to post pictures on SNS when I am traveling.

他結束旅行歸來時就立刻向朋友們講述他的旅遊經驗。
He told his friends about his travel experience as soon as he came back from his trip.

不同州（state）的銷售稅

去美國旅行時，有時在購物或餐廳用餐後要結帳時，總是會發現要付的金額比預期中高很多，因而感到困惑。為什麼要支付比價格表上標示價格更高的金額呢？

美國的銷售稅（Sales Taxes）與我們的增值稅（Value Added Tax: VAT）概念相似，但繳納方式卻有很大不同。首先，美國的銷售稅由各州政府（State Government）而非聯邦政府（Federal Government）徵收。因此，商品的最終價格必須再加收10%的銷售稅。而美國的銷售稅則依州而異，商品標示的價格未附加銷售稅，即免稅價格，實際結帳時需根據所在州的稅率額外支付銷售稅。銷售稅由兩種稅金，即銷售稅（Sales Tax）和地方稅（Local Tax）的總和計算。銷售稅由各州政府徵收，而地方稅則為地方政府的消費稅。

美國各州的銷售稅範圍相當廣泛。例如，德拉瓦州（DE）、奧勒岡州（OR）和新罕布夏州（NH）並不徵收銷售稅，因此商品的價格即為最終支付價格，相對而言可以更便宜地購買商品。因此，在美國要直接購物時，許多人更喜歡在免徵銷售稅的德拉瓦、

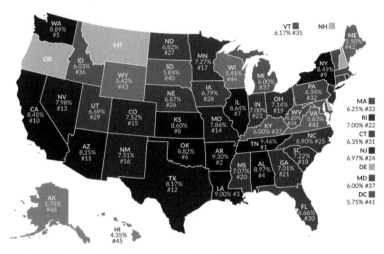

How High Are Sales Taxes in Your State?

Combined State & Average Local Sales Tax Rates, 2016

WA 8.89% #5
OR
MT
ND 6.82% #27
ID 6.03% #36
SD 5.84% #40
WY 5.42% #43
MN 7.27% #17
WI 5.41% #44
MI 6.00% #37
NV 7.98% #13
UT 6.69% #29
CO 7.52% #15
NE 6.87% #26
IA 6.79% #28
IL 8.64% #7
IN 7.00% #22
OH 7.14% #19
PA 6.34% #32
CA 8.48% #10
KS 8.60% #8
MO 7.86% #14
KY 6.00% #37
WV 6.20% #34
VA 5.63% #41
AZ 8.25% #11
NM 7.51% #16
OK 8.82% #6
AR 9.30% #2
TN 9.46% #1
NC 6.90% #25
SC 7.22% #18
TX 8.17% #12
LA 9.00% #3
MS 7.07% #20
AL 8.97% #4
GA 7.01% #21
FL 6.66% #30
AK 1.78% #46
HI 4.35% #45
VT 6.17% #35
NH
ME 5.50% #42
NY 8.49% #9

MA 6.25% #33
RI 7.00% #22
CT 6.35% #31
NJ 6.97% #24
DE
MD 6.00% #37
DC 5.75% #41

Note: City, county, and municipal rates vary. These rates are weighted by population to compute an average local tax rate. Three states levy mandatory, statewide local add-on sales taxes at the state level: California (1%), Utah (1.25%), and Virginia (1%). We include these in their state sales tax rates. The sales taxes in Hawaii, New Mexico, and South Dakota have broad bases that include many business-to-business services. Due to data limitations, the table does not include sales taxes in local resort areas in Montana. Some counties in New Jersey are not subject to statewide sales tax and collect a local rate of 3.5%. Their average local score is represented as a negative.
Source: Sales Tax Clearinghouse; Tax Foundation calculations.

Combined Sales Tax Rate
Lower   Higher

TAX FOUNDATION   @TaxFoundation

奧勒岡和新罕布夏州的商店購物，以獲得更實惠的價格。

然而，路易斯安那州（LA）、田納西州（TN）、阿肯色州（AR）和華盛頓州（WA）的情況則不同，因為消費者在購買商品時需要支付高達9%以上的銷售稅，相對而言給消費者帶來相當的負擔。

在美國購物時，特別是進行網購，須特別注意賣家所在地址，因為所在位置不同，其銷售稅的徵收標準也有所不同，因此選擇位於銷售稅較低的州的商家購物，有助於節省購物成本。

INDEX 索引

依照英文字母順序

C

E

H

台灣廣廈 國際出版集團
Taiwan Mansion International Group

國家圖書館出版品預行編目（CIP）資料

1本就通！日常英文表達大小事 / 姜鎮豪、卞惠允著.
-- 初版. -- 新北市：語研學院, 2024.02
面；　公分
ISBN 978-626-97939-3-8（平裝）
1. CST: 英語　2. CST: 會話

805.188　　　　　　　　　　　　　112018888

LA PRESS 語研學院 Language Academy Press

1本就通！日常英文表達大小事
從起床到就寢，幾乎涵蓋所有一天生活的日常用語，讓你自然養成開口說英文的原子習慣！

作　　者／姜鎮豪、卞惠允	編輯中心編輯長／伍峻宏・編輯／許加慶
譯　　者／Emma Feng	封面設計／何偉凱・內頁排版／菩薩蠻數位文化有限公司
	製版・印刷・裝訂／皇甫・秉成

行企研發中心總監／陳冠蒨　　　　　線上學習中心總監／陳冠蒨
媒體公關組／陳柔彣　　　　　　　　產品企製組／顏佑婷、江季珊、張哲剛
綜合業務組／何欣穎

發　行　人／江媛珍
法律顧問／第一國際法律事務所 余淑杏律師・北辰著作權事務所 蕭雄淋律師
出　　版／語研學院
發　　行／台灣廣廈有聲圖書有限公司
　　　　　地址：新北市235中和區中山路二段359巷7號2樓
　　　　　電話：（886）2-2225-5777・傳真：（886）2-2225-8052
讀者服務信箱／cs@booknews.com.tw

代理印務・全球總經銷／知遠文化事業有限公司
　　　　　地址：新北市222深坑區北深路三段155巷25號5樓
　　　　　電話：（886）2-2664-8800・傳真：（886）2-2664-8801
郵政劃撥／劃撥帳號：18836722
　　　　　劃撥戶名：知遠文化事業有限公司（※單次購書金額未達1000元，請另付70元郵資。）

■出版日期：2024年02月　　　　　ISBN：978-626-97939-3-8
　　　　　　　　　　　　　　　　版權所有，未經同意不得重製、轉載、翻印。